Devon Destroyers MC

(South Coast Brothers)

Kacey Hamford

To Vicky

#WIW18

K. Hamford x

Table Of Contents

Acknowledgments

First of all I would like to thank my amazing partner for supporting me in my adventure of becoming a writer. For all of the late night and early mornings that I had to get up and write the story that just wouldn't let me sleep.
I'd like to thank and mention Lucii, my PA, editor, beta reader and most importantly my friend. She keeps me motivated and on the right track.
Stephanie from SP Cover Design, for this amazing cover.
Kathleen, Laura, Claire, Emma, Titian and Natalie who are my number one fans. For their great support, advice and encouragement.
Bonnie, who helped me out greatly in this book. Without her I wouldn't have had such detail and the true way a biker club works.
My street team, Kacey's Kick Ass Crew. Without all of your support in buying and reading my books I wouldn't be where I am now. I appreciate all of your help and support in getting me and my books out there.
My beta readers, thank you for being completely honest and for all of your feedback regarding this book.
Finally, I'd like to thank all of you for buying my books and helping me on my way to my dream job of becoming an author.
Now, I'll leave you all in peace to enjoy the first instalment of the South Coast Brothers.
Happy reading.

Chapter 1

Heather

"Babe?" My husband, James, called out as he barged in through the front door. His voice sounded urgent. I walked out of the kitchen and into the hallway; our son was kicking me and I rubbed my hand over my swollen tummy. I smiled as my tattooed biker husband came into view. "You need to pack a bag." He told me.
"Pack? Why?" I was confused, he seemed agitated. He kept looking over his shoulder towards the door.
"We need to leave… Now!" He roared.
"But all the baby stuff is here…" I began but he cut me off. Did he want us to leave and never come back?
"We'll buy new stuff, we can't wait. We need to get on my bike and be gone."
"I'm eight months pregnant, I can't get on the back of your bike. What's going on?" He began pacing, running his hands over his face and through his hair.
"SHIT!" He yelled as the sounds of bikes pulled up outside of our house. "You need to go, run!"
"What have you done? I thought you were out of the bike club? You told me you went enforcer!" I cried at him.
"I did, I have. They called in a favour… Shit went down and things went wrong."
Bang. Bang. Bang.
"James! Open up we know you're in there." A man shouted.
"Who's that?" I asked as James began pushing me towards the back door.
"Uno." He stated.
"The president of the MC?" I squealed in fear, I remember him telling me he was called Uno as all it took was one shot

for him to kill someone and he never missed. He nodded. "What have you done?" I asked him again, I dug my heels into the carpet so he couldn't push me anymore. He got frustrated and picked me up and thrust the car keys into my hand.

"Get in the car and drive, go see your Mum or Sister. Just get the fuck away." He opened the back door and a large man was standing there. I yelped as I heard the front door being kicked in and before I knew it James was rolling on the floor holding onto his side. I wanted to get on the floor to see if he was ok but knew that wouldn't be easy, not in my condition. The guy that was standing in the doorway grabbed the top of my arm and pushed me to sit at the kitchen table.

"Hello, sweetheart." Uno, the president of the Devon Destroyers MC, smirked at me. He was a tall, broad man, with a graying beard and tattoos covering his arms and neck.

"What do you want?" I asked. I knew I shouldn't talk back to these guys but they had just invaded my home and I didn't have a clue what was going on.

"Your husband here has a little debt to pay… Riz, wake him up." The tall, skinny guy who had a fag hanging from his mouth pulled James off the floor and shoved him into a chair. He slapped him round the face a couple of times until he started waking up. James looked around frantically, his eyes softened when he saw me.

"Don't hurt her." He pleaded.

"Oh, we won't hurt her. We may let Ripped have a go at her though." Uno chuckled and I looked around to find a tall, muscular, tattooed bloke staring at me, he was devouring me with his eyes and it made me feel sick to my stomach.

"NO!" James called out, struggling against the guy who was holding him in his chair.

"I don't think you're in any situation to be demanding stuff." Riz growled at him, pulling at his hair on his head.

"You told me you were out of the Devon MC." I said quietly

to James. I heard a loud chuckle behind me and saw Uno had his head thrown back laughing.
"Sweetheart, he never left us... He has created us a whole load of trouble though and now he has to pay."
"What have you done?" I cried at him.
"I'm sorry, babe. I am."
"Prez." Another guy said, getting Uno's attention and all he did was nod towards me.
"Go ahead and tell her, Itch." I looked from Uno to the guy called Itch, he was staring at James and cracking his knuckles in his hand. He was thinner than the other guys, dressed all in leather and had tattoos covering his arms, neck and face. I wondered what the hell was going on.
"Your husband here... He's been fucking my wife." I gasped out of surprise and shook my head, I didn't believe him. "I caught them today, going at it on my kitchen table." He shouted and slammed his hand down on the table in front of me. I gulped as I looked at his hand, what was he going to do?
"James?" My voice trembled as I asked if it was true. He nodded his head and I couldn't fight the tears from sliding down my face. "How long?"
"Yeah, that's what we would all like to know, how long were you fucking her?" Itch roared.
"Six months." James stuttered and he was rewarded with a punch in the face from Itch. I screamed again as I wasn't used to the violence. Yeah, I knew my husband was involved with the MC, but he told me he got out over six months ago and he helped them on very rare occasions.
"You see, doll. She was a club whore." Itch started to explain. "I made her my Old Lady, that's all she wanted, she didn't care
that I fucked on the side or brought other women to bed with us. She was supposed to be faithful to me, she wore my properties, a vest telling people she was mine. She knew what the consequences of fucking another brother would be, so she

grabbed my gun and shot herself. Made it easy on herself."
"Oh, God." I sobbed.
"Now, someone has to pay." He stated, I heard a gun cock and looked around to see Uno pointing a gun at me.
"NO!" I screamed as I placed my hands over my tummy as if to protect my baby.
"I lost my wife and now he'll lose his." Itch declared.
"Hold up, I want her." Another voice said from behind all the guys, I couldn't see anyone as I looked around. What did he mean when he said he wanted me? To fuck? To claim? To hurt? A large handsome, dark haired man with stubble covering his face with a few visible tattoos stepped forward and the MC guys stood back from him apart from Uno, who still had a gun pointed at me.
"What are you doing here, Blade?" Uno asked him.
"Went to the club, they told me what went down and I wanted to join the fun." He took another step closer, knelt down in front of me and placed both of his hands on my large bump. I jumped and pressed my back further into the chair, attempting to get away from him, but failed miserably. Uno removed his gun from me and I just looked at the guy they called Blade, my little boy was going mad inside me, kicking and moving around a lot.
"Get away from my wife." James shouted, which earnt him another tug on his head.
"You claiming her?" Ripped asked.
"Fuck, I don't know, I'll have to see how she fucks." Blade snorted, he removed his hands and stood up straight. "But you ain't killing her." I jumped when I felt a hand on mine and realised it was James. I looked at him and smiled and then remembered what he'd done. He had been sleeping with another woman, maybe more than just one. I pulled my hand away from him and I saw the hurt on his face.
"Well, someone has to pay." Itch shouted as he pulled his gun out and held it to James's head.

"I love you, babe." He said to me.
"Love me?" I shouted, jumping to my feet. "Is Love sticking your dick in other women? Is love bringing this crap to my house? Putting me and my baby in danger? Fuck you." I screamed. "I hate you. Just do it." I said looking at Itch, rage coursing through my veins. I was feeling emotional and irrational all at the same time, I couldn't get my feelings under control. Did I really want him dead?
"You might wanna look away, sweetheart." Uno said from behind me. I shook my head and walked towards the chair I was sitting in.
"Just do it." I sneered at Itch. Uno let out a loud laugh and said;
"You'll make a great Old Lady."
"No chance." I said to him, I couldn't think of anything worse than having to live with guys like them, cheating and killing people.
Bang. Bang.
The gunshots made me jump and I screamed, holding onto my tummy. James slumped over the kitchen table and I couldn't take my eyes off him.
"I'll call the clean-up crew." Riz said as he walked away, talking on the phone. I got to my feet and pushed past all the men.
"Where do you think you're going, sweetheart?" Uno called out after me.
"For a lie down, I'd appreciate it if you all left."
"That's not gonna happen." He told me, I stopped walking and turned to face him. I felt a pair of hands close in on my arms and I looked behind me to see Ripped standing there. I struggled against his hold and his grip tightened. I cried out from the pain. "You have to work off his debt."
"Fuck you. I'm not working as a club whore, I'm eight fucking months pregnant... Asswipe."
"She's got a dirty mouth on her, Prez." Ripped chuckled.

"The guys at the club are gonna love her." Riz added.
"Are you insane?" I shouted, looking around at them all.
"I'll take her, we'll take her car." Blade winked, walking towards me. "Let's go and get you packed up." He took my arm from Ripped and led me towards the stairs.
"I'm not fucking you." I adamantly told him.
"Didn't ask you to, Sugar." He slapped me gently on the bum and I yelped and began climbing the stairs.
"I don't have a choice but to go, do I?" I asked Blade as he placed my suitcase on the bed and I began throwing clothes into it. I knew a little bit about the way a MC club worked, if I tried to run, I'd just be killed. No one defied them, everyone was scared of them. They were a nasty looking group of guys.
"I'm afraid not, but I'll try and keep you safe." He smiled at me. There was something different about this guy, he was gentler, kinder and not at all scary.
"And how are you going to do that?" I asked, placing my hands on my hips.
"If you become my…"
"I'm not going to be your Old Lady. I don't even know you." I said cutting him off mid-sentence.
"Fine." He shrugged his shoulders as he lent back against the bedroom wall, crossed his arms across his chest and crossed one foot in front of the other, watching me pack my clothes.
"What do I do about all the baby stuff?" I asked, looking at the moses basket that was in the corner of the room.
"What stuff?" He asked, straightening himself up.
"The moses basket, changing bag, clothes, bottles..."
"Ok, I get it… You don't need this shit yet, I'll come back for it." I nodded my head and looked longingly at it. I hoped my life or my son's life wouldn't be in danger by going into that club house.
"I'm all done. Can't I have one more night here?" I pleaded.
"Nope." He walked towards my suitcase, grabbed the handle and my hand and dragged us both down the stairs. I wanted

to fight, I wanted to scream, I wanted to run but I knew it would be no good, I wouldn't get far.

Chapter 2

Heather

I followed Blade into the Devon MC compound, it looked like an old warehouse. It was about two hours away from where we lived in Cornwall. We were now in Devon and I had never left Cornwall before.

"Come on, Sugar." Blade said as I hesitated at the door.

"Heather, my name is Heather."

"I know that, Sugar." He chuckled, carrying my suitcase and I followed him through the door. I looked behind me and there was a row of bikes all lined up and a group of bikers standing around talking. Once I walked into their vision, the cheers and cat calls started. I couldn't believe I had to live here, put up with this and I definitely didn't know how Blade was supposed to keep me safe when he was an enforcer. He belonged to the Devon MC, but he helped out several others when they needed it, too.

We walked in the main door and came straight into a bar, it was full of bikers, drinking, and women with hardly any clothes on. They must have been the club whores. Some were serving drinks, some were dancing for the guys on a stage and some were sexually pleasing them. A few of the women gave me funny looks, it was probably because I was so out of my depth being here, how did I manage to marry a no hoper who had now ruined my life.

"Follow me." Blade said as he began walking down a hall that ran alongside the bar, there were a few open doors and I spotted a kitchen. My tummy growled at the thought of food. Then I saw a room that looked like a pool room, and there was a girl tied to the pool table, spread eagled and she was being fucked by two guys, one in the mouth and one in the pussy. I quickly looked away and felt a blush rise up my cheeks.

"You'll have to get used to that, Sugar." Blade chuckled as he stopped outside of a door and unlocked it. He pushed the door open and I walked in first. The double bed was messy and unmade, there was dirty clothes all over the floor and it smelt of alcohol and sex. "This is where you'll be sleeping."

"Is this your room?" I asked, turning towards him.

"Yep, we'll have to stay in here together. At least keep up the pretence that I've claimed you, else those guys will be all over you."

"Why would they be all over me? Look at me, I'm like a beached whale."

"Pussy is pussy to them, Sugar." He shrugged his shoulders as he placed my suitcase on the bed. "You'll have to live out of this until I can make room for you."

"You're sleeping on the floor and you need to get that bed changed and tidy this room up." I demanded.

"If you don't want to sleep in it, you change it. There's clean sheets in the cupboard in the hall."

"You're gonna make me struggle to change it?" I asked, glaring at him.

"You can always sleep on the floor." He chuckled.

"You asshole. Why the hell are you doing this to me? Can't I get my own room?"

"No." He stated as he sat on the edge of the bed.

"I'm talking to Uno, he'll get me a room, a clean and tidy one."

"This ain't no hotel, Sugar. The only way to get another bed is to sleep with one of those guys out there." He said, pointing his finger towards the bar. I cringed inside at the thought of letting any of them close to me.

"Where do the club whore's sleep?"

"They're called sweet buns here, Sugar. They won't be happy hearing you call them that."

"Fine." I said rolling my eyes. "Where do they sleep?"
"They sleep in the bed of whoever chooses them for the night." He shrugged.
"What if they don't get chosen?"
"Then they have a communal room they sleep in." He told me.
I had only been to a club house a couple of times when James had to travel and we didn't want to be apart.
"Can't I stay in there?"
"Yeah, sure…" He started to say, I cut him off.
"Great." I grabbed my suitcase and attempted to lift it. Blade stopped me.
"If you want to get fucked in the middle of the night."
"What?"
"If you stay in the communal room, you'll be fair game to any of those bikers and not just to the Devon MC, any bikers who come and visit and stay."
What kind of place was this? How was I ever going to get used to living here? I was in a nightmare.
Knock. Knock. Knock.
"What?" Blade shouted out as he stood beside me and put his arm around me. The door pushed open and a small, slim blonde girl who couldn't have been more than eighteen walked into the room.
"Hi, Blade." She purred at him.
"Cammie." He said, nodding his head at her. "What do you want?"
"I've come for, Heather is it?" She looked at me and I nodded my head. "Uno wants her on stage."
"WHAT?" He bellowed.
"He said she has to start paying off her debt."
"Wait outside." He growled and she left the room. "Shut the God damn door."
"What is she talking about?" I asked. She said I had to go on stage, what was I going to have to do?
"Uno wants you to dance on stage. Strip." He ran his hands

through his short hair as if he was unhappy about this.
"Look at me." I waved my hand over my bump. "This is not a sight to see, naked. Stretch marks and varicose veins." I complained.
"It's this or sleep your debt away, besides there are a few guys that have pregnancy fetishes."
"What?" I asked looking disgusted. "I get why the baby Daddy would be turned on as he made this, but not some random guy."
"It's something to do with the baby moving while fucking." He waved his hand in the air like he didn't understand. I grabbed his hand in between mine and looked him in the eye. "Please, don't make me do this." I pleaded.
"Sugar, I can't stop this. This isn't my club. What the Prez says, goes. It's best you go before he comes and finds you." I nodded my head and opened the door to find Cammie standing there, it was for the best if I just got on with it, there was no changing what I had to do, I just had to make the best out of it. I looked around for a way to escape but I knew I wouldn't get far. I took a deep breath and followed this girl who chose to be here. Cammie led me to a small changing room and handed me an outfit, it was a bright pink bra and panty set with sequins on it.
"I have to wear this?" She nodded. "I thought I had to strip? This won't take long to get off."
"You strip down to that, Blade won't be happy if the other guys see your assets, you're not a sweet bun, but Uno said you have a debt to pay. This is the best way to do it." I nodded and she stood there staring at me. Though I wasn't sure why Blade would care so much what the guy's saw. "Do you know what to do out there?"
"Not a clue, I've never done this before… They just killed my husband and brought me here."
"Sshh." Cammie said as she placed her hand over my mouth and shook her head. "Don't talk about what you've seen.

That'll get you killed." I nodded my head and she released me. "Look as sexy as you can, dance around the pole, shake your ass and tits. Normally we wear heels, but I think you should go bare footed." I nodded again and placed my hand on my tummy, he was kicking up a storm. "Don't worry about me seeing anything, get dressed. I'll stay by the stage and if it looks like your failing I'll come and rescue you, they love a bit of girl on girl." I nodded again, I couldn't believe what I was about to do and had no words to speak. I quickly changed and Cammie led me towards the stage. I would do what I needed to do, to survive and hope that soon I'd be able to go back to my house and back to Cornwall. How much debt could James have accumulated?

Chapter 3

Blade

Uno wanted her to dance, I knew this was going to happen, he saw how I looked at her; how I wanted her for myself and by making her dance, all these guys watching would want to fuck her. For me to claim her I would have to commit completely to this club, no longer be an enforcer. He considered Heather his, now that she would be working off her husband's debt, so I couldn't just grab her and run else we would have the MC after us for the rest of our lives. Uno didn't want her for himself, he had an Old Lady, Gloria, and she satisfied him. He wasn't like the rest of them, he didn't fuck on the side; he knew that if she found out she would castrate him.

I pulled back a chair and sat at the table closest to the stage, in case there was any trouble and I needed to get her away from everyone. Uno sat opposite me, I saw him out of the corner of my eye but I didn't acknowledge that he was there.

"You sure she's worth all of this, you hardly know her." I didn't answer him, something about her called out to me; was it her vulnerability? Was it her pregnancy? "You'll need to fuck her in front of us so we know this is for real and not a way for you to save her." My head snapped to look at him.

"Fuck off, Prez. That ain't no rule I've ever heard of." He threw his head back and laughed out loud, he rose from his seat, lent over the table and said;

"She isn't Willow." I kicked my chair back and grabbed the front of his shirt.

"What the fuck you say?" I growled and he laughed in my face, I felt myself being dragged backwards and once we weren't moving I shrugged the guys off and sat back at the table.

"Ok, gentlemen, we have a treat for you tonight." Ripped started saying. "A new girl, Heather, who is eight months pregnant, enjoy." The crowd went wild and my gaze was fixed on the stage. The music started, the curtain was pulled back and there was Heather leaning against the pole, she had long wavy brown hair that fell around her shoulders, brown eyes, a row of butterfly tattoos that ran up the side of her hand and a pale complexion. She had on a short thin robe, tied around her large tummy, she swayed her hips to the beat of the song, she circled the pole once and leant her back against it, her back was towards us and she slid up and down the pole the best she could. She looked over her shoulder and her eyes connected with mine. I gave her a nod of encouragement and she walked around the pole undoing her robe, she slipped it off her shoulders and she was wearing a see through baby doll nightie, luckily she had on a pink bra and panty set. The guys were going wild, I had a table near Bump; he got his name as he was always after women with bumps; pregnancy bumps. He had his hand down his trousers and I shook my head laughing.

"Crystal!" He shouted and a bubbly blonde haired girl walked towards him, she couldn't have been more than nineteen at the most. She knew what he wanted, he pushed his chair back and she dropped to her knees in front of him and pulled his dick out of his jeans and slipped it straight into her mouth. I looked back to the stage and Heather was undoing the front of the nightie, she was getting ready to remove it, she ran her hands over her tummy and Bump slammed his hand down on his table and shouted out praise to her and the girl sucking him off. As soon as her bare expanding tummy was on show; Bump called out and pounded into the girl faster and harder, even I could hear her gagging from where I was sitting. Heather stumbled slightly and pressed her hand into her side,

I rose out of my seat and Cammie ran onto the stage, she stood in front of Heather and began dancing with her, she had her hands on Heather's tummy and they began dancing and caressing each other until the song finished. Cammie had stripped down to nothing and I was thankful that Heather still had her bra and panty set on.

Chapter 4

Heather

"What happened out there?" Cammie asked as she pulled her clothes on.

"Big kick from the baby." I told her rubbing my hand over the spot where he had kicked me.

"You can't let that happen again, Uno won't be happy." She told me.

"How often am I going to have to do this?" I asked while dressing.

"Every night, I'm guessing." She told me.

"Do you do this every night?"

"No, but I do other things..." She began saying when there was a loud banging on the door and a short rounded man with a bushy beard walked in.

"Out!" He growled at Cammie, she looked towards me and back towards this man.

"You know she's Bl..." Cammie began talking when he grabbed her by the hair and slammed her into the nearest wall. I let out a little scream.

"I said, GET OUT!" He roared in her ear. She nodded frantically and he let her go and she looked at me with an apology in her eyes. She had tried to keep this guy away from me; what did he want? Who was he? After the door slammed shut, he turned towards me. I had managed to back myself up against the wall and his eyes were fixed on my tummy.

"Who are you?" My voice trembled with fear.

"Club whores don't get to ask questions."

"But, I..." I stuttered.

"And they don't interrupt either." He growled gripping my

face painfully in his hand. He placed his hand on my tummy and his smile grew as my little boy began moving and kicking. "I'm gonna enjoy this." He chuckled. His hands moved over my tummy towards my breasts, I begged him to stop, but he carried on. I didn't want this, I didn't want to be here; I needed to find a way out. I couldn't push him off me, I was afraid of what he might do; I couldn't risk him harming my baby. I needed to find a way to contact my sister, I haven't spoken to her in a little while but the last I heard she had married a VP in a MC club, maybe he could get me out, how was I going to contact her? I knew there was no point in me fighting, I would not get away from him. I closed my mind off and waited for him to be done when I heard a large bang and then felt the guy moving away. I opened my eyes and saw that Blade had pulled him away from me, I sagged in relief and slid down the wall. I will not cry, I will not give them the satisfaction of seeing me fall apart. A few minutes later I felt a hand on my arm and I screamed out.

"Hey, it's just me… I'm sorry, I tried to get help as soon as I could." It was Cammie and she was sitting on the floor with me. I looked up at her and forced a thank you smile on my face.

"Sugar, did he hurt you?" Blade was crouched down in front of me and I looked over his shoulder and saw that the guy was flat on his back. I shook my head and Blade scooped me up in his arms and walked away.

Blade

I couldn't quite believe what Cammie was telling me, Bump had forced his way into their dressing room and threw her out so he could be alone with Heather. I knew exactly what his plan was, I turned my head towards Uno.

"Set up the church meeting, early. They need to know I'm back and she is mine." Uno smirked at me and raised his bottle of beer at me to tell me he understood. The only way I could protect Heather was to make her mine, I didn't like to be committed to one MC, but I needed to do this. My mind wandered to the past.

"Baby, nothing is gonna happen to you just because I join the MC." I assured Willow.

"There isn't just me to consider anymore." She told me placing her hand on her tummy.

"You're pregnant?" I smiled. She nodded and I grabbed her by the waist and spun her around in a circle. We had been trying for a baby for a couple of years. I knew it would happen when the time was right.

"Blade!" Cammie shouted, snapping me out of my daze. I looked at her and she had a worried look on her face, oh fuck, Heather. I ran towards the dressing room and saw that Bump had her pinned up against the wall and his hands were all over her, her head was turned to the side and she had her eyes squeezed together tightly. I grabbed him and punched him several times until he was out cold, I looked towards Heather and saw that Cammie had her arms around her. I expected her to be crying but she was just sitting there, no expression on her face. I scooped her up and walked towards my room.

"Are you ok?" I whispered as I laid her down on the bed. She didn't answer, she stared into space and rolled onto her side. I didn't know what I could do or say to make this better for her.

I paced in front of the large table at our church meeting. I was full of rage.

"I'm going enforcer." I declared.

"Brother, we can sort this out, all of us. Don't go off and do anything stupid."

"Stupid?" I roared. "You saw what they did, I need my revenge."

I snapped out of my memory when I heard Heather start to cry. I walked around the side of the bed and sat beside her.

"Hey, it's ok." I went to brush her hair off her face and she flinched. "I'm not gonna hurt you, Sugar."

"Until you want what I won't give you and then you'll just

take it. You're all the same." She sneered, wiping her tears away.

"No, I'm not like them." I told her pointing in the direction of the bar. She didn't answer me, she stared at the wall behind me. "Why are you crying?" She didn't answer me, she closed her eyes as the tears silently fell.

"They killed him." She sobbed.

"Sugar, you told them to." Her eyes snapped open to look at me.

"I was angry, I found out he had been cheating on me; he made me feel like what we had was all a lie... Doesn't mean I actually wanted him dead."

"Better him than you, Sugar. It was gonna be one of you." I told her, there was no point in sugar coating it for her, she had sat there and watched her husband get shot in the head.

"Now my baby has to grow up without his Daddy and I have to live in this place." She cried harder and buried her face into my pillow. I placed my hand on her back to comfort her and she screamed and jumped away from me. "Don't touch me." She shrieked. Her breathing was erratic and she was starting to hyperventilate.

"Sugar, that can't be good for the baby. You need to calm down."

"Just leave me alone." She panted as she struggled to breathe, closing her eyes. I stood up and left the room. I went in search for Cammie, maybe she would be able to help her, keep her calm, I didn't want her going into premature labour or anything.

I walked into the bar and looked around for Cammie, I couldn't see her so I walked up to the bar to ask Michelle.

"You seen Cammie?" She passed me a bottle of beer and I snapped it up and emptied its contents.

"She's busy with Riz, but I can help you out." She winked at me.

"Where are they?" I growled.

"Why is she so popular all of a sudden?" Michelle whined, leaning over the bar to show me her cleavage. I had fucked her a few times while I had been in town, so I knew exactly what her tits were like, fake. I hated fake.

"Where. Is. She." I demanded. She nodded her head towards the pool room and I stalked off to find her. I pushed the door open and found her riding Riz on the pool table. She was naked and his jeans were pushed down to his feet. "Cammie!" I called out and she looked up at me, not stopping her movements.

"I'll be with you in a few minutes." She winked at me, is that what she thought I was after?

"Now!" I demanded as I stormed towards her and pulled her off Riz by grabbing her arm. She yelped in surprise.

"What the fuck man? Can you not wait your turn?" Riz complained.

"I need her. Now." I shouted. "Get dressed." I told her.

"What's the point? Or you wanna undress me yourself?" She purred.

"Cammie." I said in a warning tone and she grabbed her shorts and top and slipped them on, not bothering with underwear. I grabbed her arm and pushed her out of the door ahead of me.

"Where to, handsome?" She asked as she turned around and ran her hand over my cock through my jeans. I grabbed her hand and pulled her off me.

"My room." I growled. She turned on her heel and began walking.

"So, what's the deal, you can fuck who you want but the guys aren't allowed to see Heather naked?" I ignored her questions and pushed her through my bedroom door, I nodded my head towards the bed where Heather was laying on her side, crying her eyes out. Cammie looked at me in confusion. "She won't let me near her, she needs calming down. Can you try?" I whispered to her. She nodded her head and I turned around

and left the room.
I walked back into the bar area, I needed another drink. I sat on a stool at the bar and Michelle handed me another beer, I began drinking it.
"Whiskey." I demanded. She handed me the drink, winked and walked away, I watched her ass move in that short skirt she was wearing and I felt my dick stiffen in my jeans.
"Where's your girl?" Uno asked as he sat next to me. I nodded my head towards the bedrooms and he laughed. "Not giving you what you need?"
"She's eight months pregnant, she watched her husband get shot and she was made to come here and live to pay off his debts. Do you think I'm some kind of animal? You think I'd force myself on her. I am not like some of your men." I downed the whiskey and slammed the glass on the bar, I wanted another one but Michelle had disappeared. I leant over the bar, grabbed the bottle and walked to a table at the back of the room. Uno followed me, he sat down opposite me and I took a large gulp from the bottle.
"You think you can save this one? Make up for your failures?" He questioned. I stopped drinking from the bottle as he said this. I flipped the table over and grabbed the front of his t-shirt.
"You don't know shit." I growled in his face, swaying slightly from the amount of whiskey I had consumed. He laughed as I was pulled off him by Riz and Ripped.
"You couldn't save them, you can't save her. She's ours now." He smirked and I lunged towards him. None of them would be getting their hands on her, I wouldn't let them.
"Michelle!" Ripped called out and then before I knew it Michelle had hold of my hand and was pulling me towards the toilets. Once we were inside she pushed me against the wall and stood in front of me.
"You need to calm down... You don't go up against the Prez of the MC."

"You do not tell me what to do. I tell you." I growled as I grabbed the back of her head and slammed my mouth down onto hers, thrusting my tongue into her mouth. I spun us around so I had her pressed against the wall. I was full of frustration and rage and needed to get it out. I pulled at my belt and my jeans until my cock was free, she stroked me a couple of times and I grabbed her leg and hoisted her up the wall, she wrapped her long legs around my waist. I ran my hand under her skirt and was pleased that she wasn't wearing any underwear. I grabbed her hand that was around my cock and pinned it to the wall with one of my hands. I used my other hand to hold her up under her ass and slammed my hard cock into her. She cried out and I knew it was because I was being rough, I hadn't got her ready for me, but she was already wet. I pounded into her, slamming her harder and harder against the wall, I gripped her wrist in my hand tighter and squeezed, she cried out, probably from the pain and that made me go harder and faster. I released her wrist and tore her t-shirt and bra from her body. She gripped hold of my shoulders and I bit and sucked her nipples into my mouth. She cried out again and I could feel her body squeezing me, shit; no condom. Fuck. I pulled out of her and let my release cover her body.

Chapter 5

Blade

We were all gathered around the large table in the private room that only MC brothers' were allowed in. I had to be at this meeting as I was a member of the club, I had been an enforcer, travelling around and helping out when needed for two years now. I wasn't interested in being part of a club permanently and I definitely wasn't thinking about getting an Old Lady.

"Right, first on the agenda is Blade. He's sticking around for a bit and has a claim on the new chick. I for one, am happy to accept him into our club, permanently. Welcome to the club, Blade." Uno said as he threw a leather vest at me, displaying the logo proudly on the back and my name. This is what you gave to your Old Lady. I nodded as a thank you and Uno carried on. "Agenda two, the girls down at 'Skins' have been having trouble with some of the clients, so I'm gonna need a rotation of brothers to go down there every night to keep an eye on things. We can't have our best girls leaving us. Ripper and Riz you can start tonight, sort out the days together."

'Skins' was the strip club owned by the MC, it was a good source of income and covered up any dodgy dealings we had going on.

"Agenda three, we have a shipment coming in. I'm gonna need two guys to transport it to The Bear Devils MC. Itch and Blade you'll run this one."

"Prez, The Bear Devils is over six hours away, I don't wanna leave my girl so soon to her arriving."

"She'll be fine. Final agenda, CG I want you to find out everything you can about her, I don't want any surprise visitors looking for her. That's it, get to work." Prez slammed

the gavel on the table and all the guys got up and left, I stayed in my seat and Uno looked at me, eyebrows high on his head. "Got something to say, brother?"
"I'm not happy about the shipment, you know how I feel about drugs... After..."
"I know what happened to her, you need to get over it, move on. You want to claim that lady in there, you be a part of this family." I nodded and rose from my seat. "Now you're an official brother, get the tattoo. Jake can do it..."
"I've got a tattooist, I'll get it done this morning before we head off." I cut him off. He nodded and left the room. I followed him out and towards the bar, I needed to see Heather. I left her and Cammie to it last night and went back to my house.
"Hey, Blade." Michelle purred as she walked up to me. I didn't want to deal with this shit this morning, I had too much on my mind and needed to get to Heather. "I gathered your seed that you poured over me last night and pushed it back into my body. Maybe we'll have a baby soon." My head snapped towards her and I pushed her into the closest wall my hand closing around her throat.
"I better have just heard you wrong. Did I?" She shook her head slightly, she couldn't move much from the grip I had on her. Her face was growing red and I took a step closer to her. "If you end up pregnant with my baby by stealing my sperm, you are dead once it's born." Her hands were clawing at my hand and I loosened my grip and threw her to the floor. I turned around and Heather was standing there watching me. "Let's go." I said walking towards her holding my hand out for her and she took a step back. "NOW!" I roared. She jumped and quickly placed her hand in mine. I ran my thumb over the back of her hand in a soothing gesture and she seemed to relax slightly. I pulled on her hand and we walked towards the exit of the club house.
"Where you taking her?" Ripped asked, standing in front of

us, stopping us from leaving. "If you don't bring her back, she's dead."

"I know that, I'm taking her with me to get my tattoo done. We'll be back. I got that run to do this afternoon." Ripped, the VP of the MC nodded his head for me to follow him, I let go of Heathers hand and followed him.

"Don't tell her shit, if she don't know anything no one can hurt her, I think that was your mistake the last time. She knew too much." Ripped spoke in a low tone so Heather couldn't hear us. I had always wondered if I hadn't told Willow anything, would she still be alive? I nodded my head and he slapped me on the back. "You gotta show the guys that she's yours too." He nodded his head and a couple of the guys were staring at Heather, they wanted to fuck her. "See you later, brother." I walked back towards Heather and pulled her close to me as I claimed her mouth. She pushed against my chest and I turned her body around so no one could see her trying to push me away. When we broke apart I quickly said; "I'm showing them that you're not available, it's just a kiss. Now, kiss me properly." She looked over her shoulder and the whole club was watching us. She stepped as close to me as her tummy would let her and she wound her arms around my neck and stood on her tiptoes. I held onto her hips as I didn't want her losing her balance, after a couple of minutes we broke apart laughing as the baby was kicking us both. "Come on, Sugar." We walked hand in hand to her car and climbed in.

"I can drive you know. It is my car." She said as I reversed out of the parking space. She looked happier today, maybe her little breakdown last night done her some good.

"I'm sure you can, Sugar." I chuckled.

"Where are we going?" She asked, running her hand over her baby bump.

"Is he kicking?" I asked, gesturing towards her tummy.

"Yeah, you wanna feel?" She smiled. I shook my head and

kept my eyes on the road. "So, where are we going?"

"Cornwall." I answered.

"Are we going to get the rest of my stuff?" She asked, sitting up straighter in her seat.

"Yeah, we can swing by there on the way back if you want."

"Yes, thank you... Um... Am... Um..."

"Spit it out, Sugar."

"Will I be staying in your room?" I glanced at her and she was looking down at her hands.

"Yeah, until you either work off your debt or marry me." Her head snapped up.

"Marry you? I'm already married, and by the looks of that ring so are you."

Shit. I always took my wedding ring off before I entered the club house, yesterday when I arrived there and Bump had told me what was going down I was in a rush to see what all the fuss was about and forgot I was wearing it.

"Your husband is dead." I stated.

"And where is your wife? Is she happy about you staying with me?"

"She's dead."

Chapter 6

Heather

We drove from Hope Cove in Devon to Cornwall, I missed being here and being by the sea, maybe I could convince Blade to stop off at the beach for an hour. We headed for Portwrinkle and the views around us took my breath away.
"Can we stop at the beach?" I asked.
"Sorry, Sugar, we don't have time." Disappointment coursed through my body and my emotions had me feeling like I wanted to cry. We passed by the beach and a few minutes later we pulled down a small lane and I was surprised to see that we were at the Cornish Crusaders MC club house.
"Oh my God." I called out excitedly. "What are we doing here?"
"I've gotta get some ink done; Tat is the best." He said as he climbed out of the car. I pushed my door open and he was there ready to help me climb out.
"Tat?" I asked.
"Yeah, his name is Trent, but we call him Tat for short as he's a tattooist... How do you know about this place?"
"My sister is married to the VP. I haven't seen her for years." I smiled, I was excited to see her. Blade took my hand and led me around the side of the club house towards a smaller building. It was a small tattoo shop; Blade pushed the door open and we walked inside.
"Blade, how you doing, man?" A large, tattooed man walked around the counter and pulled Blade in for a hug, causing him to let my hand go.
"I'm doing great, need some new ink." He told him.
"Oh yeah? What you need?"

"This." Blade turned around to show Tat the Devon MC logo on his cut. It was the front of a motorbike surrounded in flames, with the Devon Destroyers MC banner on it.

"You're a Devon Destroyer now?"

"Yeah, it's a long story." He chuckled.

"I'm going to go and find Daisy." I interrupted them talking.

"And who is this lovely lady?" Tat asked, looking me up and down.

"She's mine. Her name's Heather."

"Nice work, man." They did a knuckle bump thing and Blade turned to me.

"You can't go wandering around by yourself, you're still at an MC compound, they'll think your fair game."

"Give me your cut and then they'll know I'm taken."

"No, Sugar. We'll go and find her in a minute. Let me get this done first." He took his jacket off and began undoing his shirt, I wanted to see what lay underneath. He cleared his throat. Shit, I was caught staring.

"Isn't it best if I go and find her now? Then I'll have more time with her. Please?" I begged.

"How about I give her a call and tell her to come here? No one will touch her with Daisy by her side."

"Yeah, ok." Blade agreed.

"Thank you." I beamed at him. We heard Tat on the phone and once he had hung up Blade finished undressing and he walked through to the back room, I followed him and was surprised at how clean and tidy everything was.

"Hey, Tat." Daisy called out as she walked through the door, I flew to the reception area and stood in front of her.

"Heather?" I nodded and we screamed as we cuddled. I hadn't seen her for a few years. Not since I had married James and we had husbands in different MC clubs. "Oh my God, look at you. When are you due?"

"In about six weeks." I told her running my hand over my tummy.

"Where's James? Getting some ink?" She asked as she walked past me and into the back room. "Who are you?" She asked.
"Blade. Nice to meet you, Daisy." He said as Tat was working on his back, Blade was sat on a chair backwards, his arms laying on the top.
"Where's James?" Daisy asked turning back to me. I looked at Blade and he shook his head.
"Dead, I don't wanna talk about it. Where's your gorgeous husband?"
"Up at the club house. Come on." She took my hand and I looked over to Blade and he smiled and waved at me.
"I'll come find you when I'm done." He called after me. We slowly walked up to the club house, it was light and bright inside, nothing like the Devon MC.
"You want a drink?" I nodded as I sat down at a table, resting my aching feet. "Hey, Holes?" She shouted over the bar and a tall, tattooed and pierced bloke stood up. "Can we get a couple of cokes please?"
"Sure." He looked up to see who else Daisy had with her and his eyes zeroed in on me. "Heather?" I nodded and he walked over towards me.
"Oh yeah, I forgot you two knew each other." Daisy said, sounding bored.
"Knew each other?" He said looking at Daisy. "We were in love."
"Yeah, until you ran off and joined an MC." I sighed. How different would my life had been if he had never left me? Or I agreed to stay with him while he was a prospect?
"I asked you to come with me." He said as he took hold of my hand. "Oh, I see you're married." I stood up. "Whoa and a very large bun in the oven." I giggled and he stepped closer to me, giving me a hug.
"Yo, dude. Get your hands off my girl." Blade shouted as he walked into the club house. Mason, who now apparently went by the name holes, let go of me and stood back.

"Oh, so this is the husband?" He asked. I went to answer him when Blade said;
"Yes."
"Wait…" I started saying when Blade put his arm around my waist and pulled me close to him.
"Sugar, we need everyone to believe you are mine, else this won't work." I nodded and he kissed me quickly.
"What the fuck is a Devon Destroyer brother doing here in my club house?" Someone shouted. I turned around and saw Ryan standing there, Daisy's husband.
"Hitch." Blade said as he nodded his head. "Needed some ink."
"You don't have your own tattooist?" Daisy walked over towards him and he pulled her close and devoured her mouth for everyone to see. Daisy was twenty nine, two years older than me but I was always the one that acted more mature.
"Not one that's as good as Tat."
"Everyone get out, I want a word with Blade." Ryan shouted. I didn't move and Daisy pulled at my hand, I looked at Blade and he nodded his head. We walked outside and sat on a bench in the sun.
"It was great seeing you, Heather." Mason said as he pulled me to my feet. He held me close and whispered in my ear;
"The biggest mistake I ever made was letting you go." As he pulled back we looked at each other in the eyes. He was being serious, I wanted to say something but I didn't know what.
"Let's go, Sugar." Blade called out and I snapped out of my daze. I hugged Daisy goodbye and we said we would try and meet up soon.
The journey back to the Devon MC was quiet, I wanted to know what Ryan had said to Blade, but I knew he wouldn't tell me. I also couldn't get out of my head what Mason had said to me. We were nearing where my house was.
"Can we stop and get my stuff for the baby?" I asked, sitting up straighter in my seat.

"Not today, Sugar. No time left." Disappointment coursed through my body and I leant my head against the window wondering how different my life would be if James had never got involved with the MC. I hated that he betrayed me, it almost made me feel like I couldn't grieve for him as he hurt me so much. I never thought James would be a cheater, it just showed how little I knew about him and here I was trusting another man I knew absolutely nothing about.

Chapter 7

Blade

"How long are you going to be gone for?" Heather asked, sitting on the bed and watching as I packed some supplies in a small bag.

"Not sure."

"What am I supposed to do whilst you're gone?"

"You'll probably have to work, Sugar." I told her, she looked at me confused. "Dancing."

"Oh." She bowed her head, I crouched down in front of her and pushed at her chin. She had tears running down her face.

"What's this for?" I asked, wiping the tears away.

"What… What if the same happens as before? With Bump? What if he tries..?"

"He won't. The guys know you're mine, if anyone touches you they'll be dead. Ok?" She nodded her head and I stood up and grabbed my jacket to slip on and grabbed her hand. "You best walk me to my bike."

"Why?" She asked letting go of my hand.

"Sugar, have you never done the whole MC thing before?"

"Not really, James was in this MC for a little while but I was kept out of it. We had our own house I lived in."

"You have to come and say goodbye, for everyone to see." She nodded at me and slipped her hand into mine.

"What is it that you're doing?" She asked.

"Sugar, one thing you should know and stick to is not to ask questions. It's club business."

"Do the Old Ladies get to know?" She asked as I pulled the bedroom door open.

"Nope. Just the brothers, like I said, club business." She

nodded and we walked through the bar that was starting to fill up with people. Michelle was working behind the bar and I noticed that she had an angry looking mark around her neck. I kind of felt bad for doing that but no one and I mean no one would ever trick me into being a baby Daddy. We walked outside and Itch was already on his bike waiting for me, I climbed on my Harley Davidson Heritage Softail; it was bright blue with silver flames running down the side, as soon as I saw it I knew it was going to be mine. I pulled Heather close to me.

"Be good, don't get into trouble. Do as you're told and make sure people know that you're mine. Stick to Cammie; she's the nicest one out of them all." I whispered in her ear, she nodded and I claimed her mouth for all to see. Uno and a few other club members were outside, so I made sure that everyone knew she was mine. When we pulled apart, I looked her in the eye and wasn't sure what I saw, was it lust? Confusion? Or upset?

"Have fun. See you soon." She said quietly. I smiled at her and pulled my helmet over my head, I nodded at Itch and we took off out of the compound and on our way to the Bear Devils MC.

Heather

I felt a little lost, I didn't really know what to do with myself. I didn't want to just sit around and wait for Blade to come back. I headed towards the kitchen and pushed the door open.

"OUT!" Someone shouted and I looked up to see Uno had a woman pressed against the table and he was pounding into her from behind.

"Sorry." I said quickly as I closed the door and made my way back to the bar area. Cammie was sitting at a table with a couple of men and I didn't want to make my way over there in case they expected something. She must have seen me as

she waved me over, I walked over slowly, preparing myself to turn these guys down if they wanted something from me.
"Hi." I said as I approached the table.
"Sit down, sweetheart." One guy said as he pushed a chair out for me with his foot. I smiled at him and sat down in the chair, it was nice to get off my feet. They were starting to ache and my ankles were swelling slightly now too. The joys of being pregnant.
"Heather, this is CG…" Cammie started.
"Neil, is my name." He said as he held his hand out to shake mine. He didn't look like a typical biker, he was skinny, had short dark hair and no visible tattoos or piercings.
"Are you in the MC?" I asked. He laughed out loud and nodded his head.
"Yeah, sweetheart. I'm the brains of the club." He looked at me and I must have looked confused as he carried on with;
"CG is my nickname as I'm the computer geek."
"And this is Riz." Cammie told me, I recognised this guy as he was at my house when my husband got killed.
"Riz?" I asked.
"Yeah, Riz, as in short for Rizla." He told me, like as if I should automatically know what that meant.
"He's always smoking, whatever he's doing. Only time he doesn't smoke is when he's asleep." Cammie elaborated for me. I nodded in understanding.
"What can I do around here?" I asked, looking around. My original plan was to see if they needed help in the kitchen with cooking or cleaning but that was soon put to a halt.
"I have a suggestion what you can do." Riz smirked as he began undoing his jeans.
"She's Blades. You know that." Cammie said. "I'm free though." She winked at him and her hand disappeared into his jeans and he groaned. I jumped up from the table, I didn't want to witness that, I must have stood up too fast as my head spun and I had to grab hold of the table to stop myself from

falling.
"Whoa, sweetheart, you ok?" Neil asked as he stood beside me.
I shook my head. "Don't feel so good." I felt sick and dizzy.
"Let's sit you down." He led me to another table. "Michelle, can we get some water please?" He called out. I looked up as I heard someone approaching and Michelle was walking towards us with a jug of water in her hand and she was smiling too. Maybe I could try and make some friends while I was here, Cammie was lovely, so maybe the other girls would be too. I went to say thank you for the water when she poured it all over my head. I jumped up and screamed, I was soaked.
"That's for what your guy did to me." She sneered.
"I… I had nothing to do with that." I was standing in wet jeans, my t-shirt had now clung to my breasts and large tummy.
"Chelle, what the hell are you doing?" A woman shouted, I looked over Michelle's shoulder and a lady in her early forties walked towards us, she was beautiful with shoulder length blonde hair with a slim body, she was wearing a leather vest and she gave off a vibe of not to be messed with. Michelle didn't answer her, she went to walk away when the woman grabbed her arm. "Well?"
"Her guy done this to me." She pointed at her throat.
"That's not her fault if he gets a little rough during sex." She said, not letting her go.
"He did it this morning not last night." She explained. Last night? Does that mean Blade was with Michelle while I was having a breakdown? Why did I feel betrayed by that? He wasn't mine, not officially, we were just pretending. So why did I feel like I was about to burst into tears?
"Go and get yourself cleaned up, sweetie." I snapped out of my questioning mind and looked at this woman being nice to me. "By the way, I'm Gloria. Uno's Old Lady." I nodded and walked away to get myself cleaned up.

Chapter 8

Blade

We had been riding for over four hours and I was feeling the strain on my body, Itch and I had decided we would travel the whole way without stopping as we were both keen to get back to the club house as soon as possible. I saw a flash of light in my side mirror and as I took a closer look I noticed a large black van and a couple of motor bikes. Something about them seemed off and I spoke to Itch over our speakers that we had in our helmets.
"Incoming." Was all I said and I noticed Itch looking in his mirror.
"Let's slow down and see if they pass." He suggested. I eased off and saw the bikes and van getting closer and closer but they didn't seem to be over taking us.
"They've slowed down too." I told him, he was riding in front of me, so I had a better view of the guys behind us.
"Follow me." Itch said as he indicated and took a sharp left turning. I followed him and as we turned the corner we sped up again to try and lose them if they had followed us too.
"The van is right behind us." I announced. Who the hell was it and what did they want?
"Do a u-turn." He said as he swung his bike around and headed for the van. I followed him, the van wouldn't have been able to turn as quickly as us, being that we were now on a narrower road. As Itch got closer to the van I saw the van heading for him and Itch had to swerve which threw his bike out from under him, I was at his side within minutes, pulling him up. I looked towards the van and it had carried on but we were now faced with three bikers, gaining on us. I grabbed

Itch by the arm to help him up.
"Fuck, my tyre is burst." He shouted. I looked up and saw the bikes headed for us.
"Shit, we gotta get out of here. It's the Satan MC." Itch's head snapped up and all we saw was three bikes headed for us. Before I knew it they had started shooting. What the fuck. Itch jumped on the back of my bike and I took off down the road over the bank and headed towards the woods.
"We need to find somewhere to stop, the shipment is strapped to my bike." Itch said through the speakers in our helmets. I found a place to stop, we couldn't hear any more vehicles so we waited for the coast to be clear. Itch climbed off my bike, removing his helmet. "Shit, you're bleeding." He pointed towards my arm, I felt a sting there earlier but didn't give it another thought. "Have you been shot?" I pulled my helmet off and slipped my arm out of my cut and saw the blood pouring down my arm.
"I've just been skimmed by a bullet." I grabbed the bottom of my t-shirt and ripped it, so I could wrap and tie it around my arm. "It'll be ok once the bleeding stops." Itch nodded at me.
"Let's get back to my bike." I nodded and slipped my helmet back on as he climbed back onto my bike. I rode slowly to the edge of the woods, looking around to make sure they had gone.
"It's all clear." I said as I sped towards where Itch's bike was on its side on the side of the road. I pulled up and Itch jumped off, removing his helmet.
"Fuck, they stole the shipment and bashed my bike up." Itch's face was red, he was not happy that his bike had been messed with. I shook my head, the first job I had been on and I'd already failed.
"Let's get back and CG can sort out getting your bike collected tomorrow." Itch nodded and climbed back on my bike for the long four hour journey home.

Heather

After I had dried myself and changed my clothes, I gave myself a pep talk; to stick up for myself, if they saw me as weak then they would treat me that way. As far as everyone knew I was closing in on being an Old Lady, which meant the club whores couldn't treat me this way, they had to show some respect for us. We were the ones the guys chose to be with.

I didn't have to dance, a lot of the guys ventured out to the club 'Skins' so there were only a few guys left. Cammie was busy working and I spent most of the evening with CG - Neil. I'd learnt that he was the son of Uno and Gloria and had grown up in the club. He had patched in when he was sixteen, he was now twenty four. He wasn't in to the whole biker fiasco; drinking and fucking whores. He was much quieter and almost seemed like he didn't belong here. He said he patched in to make his Dad proud, but he always felt second best to Ripped, the club VP.

"Shouldn't you be the VP as you're the Prez's son?" I asked, taking a sip of my water.

"Na, it doesn't work like that. The Prez gets to choose."

"Well, looky over here, don't you two look cosy." Uno slurred as he fell into the seat opposite us. Neil shook his head and we both waited to see what he wanted. "Blade won't be happy if you're moving in on his girl."

"I'm not moving in on her. We're just talking, we're friends." Neil said as he relaxed in his chair, stretching his legs out in front of him.

"Friends? You can't be friends with a hot chick, you'll just wanna bang her eventually."

"Dad!" Neil scolded him.

"What? You can't tell me that if she offered it to you, you wouldn't fuck her?" He slurred, taking another gulp from the bottle in his hand.

"You're drunk. Where's Mum?" Neil asked, placing his elbows on the table, looking around for her.
"She's recovering, from the fu…"
"Ok, Dad. We get it." He cringed, raising his hand in the air stopping him from talking.
"I'm gonna head to bed." I said, yawning.
"I'll walk you." Neil said as he stood up and offered me his hand. I smiled and placed my hand in his as he helped me up. He released my hand as we began walking.
"Thank you for keeping me company tonight." I said as we walked towards Blade's room.
"It's nice to have a friend here." Neil said, quietly.
"You don't get on with them?" I asked, nodding my head towards the direction of the bar.
"Yeah, but I wouldn't call them my friends and the sweet buns just think you want sex. I don't touch them."
"Oh?"
"I'm not a typical biker." He smiled.
"Do you ride?" I asked, I loved riding on the back of James's bike, but I wouldn't want one of my own.
"Yeah, I have a car as well though." We stopped outside of Blade's room and the door was opened slightly. "Is Blade back?"
"He shouldn't be." My body perked up at the thought that Blade was home early. But why was he? Had something happened? Had something gone wrong? My happiness soon turned to worry and I pushed the door open.
"Who the fuck are you?" I screamed. There was a naked, overly skinny, red haired woman laid on my bed.
"I'm here for Blade." She slurred, rubbing her thighs together. "You joining us?" She smirked.
I stormed over to her, grabbed a fistful of her hair and yanked her off the bed. She screamed in surprise and I shoved her towards the door where Neil was standing. He caught her before she fell over, she was drunk, stoned or both.

"Get the fuck out." I sneered at her. "Don't come back, Blade is mine."
"Willow?" She asked, looking at me with a confused expression.
"Come on, Roxy, let's get you out of here." Neil said as he pushed her towards the door. I followed behind them. "Where are you going?" He asked, looking at me.
"Um… I need clean sheets." He nodded in understanding and he grabbed a clean sheet and duvet cover for me from the cupboard in the hall.
"I'll be back to help you." He told me.
"It's ok, I can do it." I assured him. He nodded again, smiled and walked away pushing Roxy in front of him.

***

I was just about to fall asleep when I felt the bed dip, I screamed and jumped off the bed. I turned the light on to see Blade lying on the bed.
"What are you doing? You scared the crap out of me." I said, placing my hand over my heart that was beating erratically.
"Nice to see you too, Sugar." He chuckled running his hands over his face and that's when I saw his arm, it was bandaged and covered in blood.
"What happened to your arm? Why are you back so early?" I asked, edging myself closer to the bed.
"Club business." Was all he said. He jumped off the bed and began pulling his clothes off, throwing them onto the floor.
"What are you doing?" I felt a slight tremble move through me, was he finally going to take what he wanted without my permission?
"Having a shower." He sounded exhausted, he stripped down to his boxers and he had a tattooed and toned body. No piercings from what I could see. His hands went to his boxers and my eyes grew wide, was he really going to strip naked in front of me. I didn't want to see him naked, or did I? I heard

him chuckle as he walked past me, still in his boxers. He stopped before he entered the bathroom, leaned towards me and whispered in my ear;

"If I didn't know any better I'd say you wanted to see underneath my boxers." I gasped in surprise, how did he know me so well already? Was I that easy to read? I shook my head and he chuckled again as he closed the bathroom door.

I sat on the edge of the bed, my little boy had woken up and he was pressed against my bladder. I just needed to wait for Blade to be finished in the shower and then I could use the toilet.

How long did it take for one person to shower? He was a man for christ sake, James used to be in and out in five minutes. Blade had already been twenty minutes. I walked over to the door and knocked on it.

"Blade, how much longer are you going to be? I need the toilet." I called out.

"Come on in, Sugar. It's not locked." He called out.

"What? No, I'm not peeing with you in there. Do you really want me to go out in the club house and use the toilet?"

"No, fine, I'm getting out." I was glad my bluff had worked, I didn't want to go out into the club house; God knows what I would have stumbled across. I heard the door click open and I climbed to my feet, Blade walked out with a towel wrapped around his waist, droplets of water still running from his hair down his toned pecs and abs. I tried to look away but I couldn't, all I kept thinking was that I wanted to run my tongue over his wet body. "Sugar?" I snapped out of my daze and look at Blade. "Don't you need the toilet?" I nodded my head and walked past him, shutting and locking the bathroom door. What had got into me? Was it my pregnancy hormones? I've never been one to devour a man with my eyes, but I couldn't look in any other direction apart from his body. I'm glad he snapped me out of my thoughts, I could see it now, me throwing myself at him, begging for him to make me come. That wasn't what I wanted, was it? I shook my head, disappointed in myself for thinking and feeling this way. I washed my hands and walked back into the bedroom, I stopped in the doorway when I saw that Blade was laying in the bed, topless.

"What are you doing?" I asked.

"Going to sleep." He answered, raising an arm above his head and getting comfy. "Did you change the bedding?"

"Yes, you had a little visitor on the bed when I came back this evening." I pulled out the spare duvet and blanket and arranged them on the floor, where it looked like I was sleeping for the night.

"Vicky?" He asked.

"No, Roxy. Should I expect more visitors?" I asked as I climbed onto the floor and attempted to get comfy.

"What are you doing?" He asked. I looked over my shoulder and he was sitting up in bed looking at me.

"Trying to sleep, can you turn the light off, please?" I moved around a bit more until I was comfy, I closed my eyes and tried to imagine I was sleeping in a nice warm and cosy bed. I heard movement from the bed and the next thing I knew I was being lifted into the air. I yelped in surprise and Blade placed me in the bed.

"Sugar, we're both adults. We can sleep in the same bed together." He placed a quick kiss on my lips, flipped off the light switch and climbed in beside me. I felt my body tense and Blade must have noticed it too. "Relax." He whispered in my ear. "I won't touch you, not until you're begging me to."

"You'll be waiting a long time then." I giggled. I felt his breath on my neck and my nipples hardened. Thank God the light was off and he couldn't see the effect he had on my body.

"There are obviously loads of women around here that want you..."

"I only want you." He whispered against my neck, causing a shiver down my spine.

"So, you haven't been sleeping with other women?" Shit, why did I ask that? I knew the answer, Michelle had said so.
"No other women. Only you." He placed a kiss on my neck and I moved away.
"Don't lie to me." I whispered into the dark room, the only sound to be heard was the ticking of a nearby clock. "I get that you can't tell me club business. But do not lie to me. That's what he had done for over six months or maybe more."
"I'm not lying."
"Oh? And what about Michelle? She told us all about your night together." I said, feeling angry.
"Fuck, I forgot about that. I was drunk and…"
"Just forget it, I don't have a claim on you, but I won't sleep with you if you are fucking other women, especially the club whores."
"Sugar, I…"
"Just don't lie to me, ever." I cut him off. I rolled onto my side, ending the conversation. I heard him sigh and felt him roll away from me.

Chapter 9

Blade

I woke up feeling warm and my arm was aching. Then I remembered that bullet skimming my arm, the bleeding had stopped after a little while, luckily I didn't need stitches. As I opened my eyes I realised why I was feeling so hot, Heather had wrapped herself around me, she had her leg over mine and her knee was pressed dangerously close to my balls. Her baby bump was pressed against my side, her bed t-shirt had risen up so we were touching skin on skin and I could feel her son kicking me. She looked beautiful sleeping in the bed next to me, I longed to reach out and touch her but knew that she would shy away from me. I needed to take a piss really bad, so I slid out of bed and walked into the bathroom. Once I was done, I walked back into the bedroom and noticed that she was now awake. I grabbed a pair of jeans and a t-shirt out of my drawer and began throwing them on.
"You in a rush to get away from me today?" She giggled. I loved that sound, I looked over and she was sitting up in bed, her hair was a mess and she had sleep lines on her face. Her hand was moving over her bump gently as if she was trying to soothe him back to sleep.
"Got club business to attend to this morning, Sugar." I winked at her.
"Ok, I'm gonna have a shower and then get some breakfast. Will Neil be at the meeting?"
"Neil?" I asked, raising my eyebrows. I didn't know she was friends with CG.
"Yeah CG. Neil's his name. What's your name?"
"I know who Neil is, Sugar. I just didn't realise you were friends."

"He looked after me last night, after Michelle threw the water over me." She shrugged her shoulders.
"Michelle did what?" I growled.
"Yeah, she threw a jug of water over me, apparently because you caused those marks around her throat."
"I'll sort this." I said as I walked towards her.
"No, don't. I need to stand up for myself else they will keep walking all over me. It was fine, Gloria sorted it."
"Gloria?" I was surprised she stepped in.
"Yeah, she is…" I gave her a look. "Oh, you know who Gloria is." She waved her hand in the air.
"Did you have to dance last night?" I asked as I sat on the edge of the bed and held her hand. She shook her head.
" A lot of the guys went to the strip club. So it was quite quiet here."
"Don't get used to it. There's a big party here this weekend, it's CG's twenty fifth birthday. Lot's of members from different clubs coming in. You may have to dance." She nodded her head. "You don't mind?"
"I can't do anything about it, the sooner I work off his debts the better."
Bang. Bang. Bang.
Someone had banged on the door so loud I thought it was going to come off the hinges.
"CHURCH." Riz called out.
"I gotta go, Sugar. See you in a little while." I leant forward and kissed her on the lips, I wanted to savour her taste, string out the kiss but knew I had to get going.
"Bye." She said quietly and I threw a wink over my shoulder to her as I left the room.

***

We had been sitting in the church meeting for over an hour and Uno was still going off on one about us being ambushed yesterday.

"What club was it?" He asked.
"Satan MC." I answered. "How did they know where we were? What we had?"
"This is what I'm trying to figure out." Uno answered. "CG, find out who was around when the guys left. Who knew where they were going and what to do. Heather?"
"No." Me and CG called out at the same time. CG cleared his throat and his focus went back to his laptop.
"Heather didn't know anything. I told her it was club business and she would never know what was going on." Uno nodded at me. "Besides the only other club she knows are the Cornish Crusaders MC, her sister is married to the VP."
"Hmm, interesting. They're coming in this weekend for the party, along with the Bear Devils, let's hope we can smooth things over with them before that." I nodded. Uno was still in deep thought as we all sat there. "CG lets chat, everyone else. OUT!"
We all scrambled to our feet and left the room, I headed for my room to see if Heather was out of bed yet. As I passed the kitchen, I heard her laugh and that stopped me in my tracks. I walked through the door and there was a mess everywhere, flour all over the worktops and on the floor and various bowls, cutlery and food were scattered along the side.
"What's all this?" I asked. She stopped stirring the bowl in her hand and looked up at me.
"Me and Cammie are making Neil a birthday cake. It's a surprise." She smiled.
"Look at this mess, if Gloria sees this…"
"I know what's going on." Gloria said as she entered the kitchen, cutting me off. I leant down and gave her a kiss on the cheek. She was always kind to me when I stayed here and it wouldn't have been a bad thing if she and Heather got along. Then I'd know that would be one person protecting her, watching her back.

Chapter 10

Heather

What was I supposed to wear to a biker birthday bash? I had dug out all of my dresses that were stuffed in my suitcase, they were all creased and I was going to look awful. I slumped onto the bed as I heard the door open.

"What happened in here?" Blade asked, chuckling to himself.

"I've got nothing to wear." I pouted as I leant up on my elbows to look at him.

"Sugar, it looks like you have lots to wear." He pointed to all the clothes that surrounded me.

"They're all creased, they have been stuffed in my suitcase."

"Shit, sorry, Sugar. I'll sort you out some space, soon."

"That doesn't help me now." I snapped. Blade walked towards me and crouched down in front of me. "I'm sorry, I just don't know what to wear."

"Just don't dress like a club whore… Oh and wear red…"

"Red? Why are you wearing red?" I cut him off.

"Oh, CG thought a theme would be good, so he went with a traffic light party."

" A traffic light party?" I asked. "Why wasn't I told?"

"Yeah, a party where if you are taken you wear red, if it's complicated you wear orange and if you are single you wear green."

"I don't have anything red to wear." I shouted. I was annoyed that I wasn't told, what would happen if I went not in the correct colour? Would I be fair game to everyone?

"That's red." He said pointing over my shoulder. I looked behind me, he was pointing at a red dress I've had forever.

"I don't think that will fit me and if it does it'll be very short."

"Just try it on." He said. I huffed and grabbed the dress and walked into the bathroom. I pulled the dress over my head and tugged it down over my expanding tummy. Luckily, the material was stretchy. It clung to all of my curves and I hated to admit it but it looked good. It was short, but I wouldn't look out of place that's for sure.

"Come on, Sugar. We're missing valuable drinking time." I pulled open the door and looked at him.

"Valuable drinking time? I can't drink." I placed my hands on my hips and stared at him. "What?" I asked as he kept quiet and stared at me. Before I knew it, he had me pressed up against the bedroom wall and he was kissing me like it was the last thing he would ever do. A hot sensation zapped around my body, my legs grew weak and I held onto his arms as he cradled my face. Our tongues entwining together, creating a dampness between my legs. When we pulled apart Blade kept his eyes shut and I could feel his hot breath against my cheek, he dropped his head to my shoulder and let out a deep breath.

"Fuck, Sugar, I couldn't stop myself." I giggled and he pulled back, looking at me. "You're not mad?"

I shook my head and pulled my bottom lip in between my teeth. "Fuck, don't do that, else we won't make it out of this room." I pushed at his chest and walked back into the bathroom to check my make-up and hair. I was glad that I put on my everlasting lipstick, if that was what he was going to be like tonight. My body was still on fire but I put that down to pregnancy hormones. I remember the beginning of my pregnancy all I wanted was sex and I was constantly horny, and while James was fucking me he was also fucking someone else. I shook my head, how could I have not seen that? What a laugh they must have been having behind my back, no wonder he went looking for someone else knowing I was going to get fat and be limited to what I could do in the bedroom.

"Sugar?" Blade called out, snapping me out of my daze. I looked up to his smiling face, I couldn't change the past all I had was the future to look forward to and on cue that's when I got a good hard kick from my little baby boy.
"I'm ready." I smiled at him, he held his hand out for me and I slipped my feet into my nude heels and placed my hand in his.
"Oh shit." He exclaimed.
"What's wrong?" I stopped to look up at him.
"You're wearing fuck me heels."
"Am I?" I asked, trying to look innocent. He threw his head back and laughed. We walked into the party that was in full swing, hand in hand. Neil had requested that none of us work the stage tonight, that some of the girls from 'Skins' were brought in and I was very thankful for that. I hated dancing for the twenty guys that were around the other night, let alone the nearly seventy that were already here.
The place was packed and all I saw were lots of green outfits. Blade pulled me towards the bar. "What do you want to drink, Sugar?" He whispered in my ear.
"Water, please." I smiled. He nodded and stood patiently waiting for his turn to be served, it felt like we had been standing here for ages, I looked over his shoulder and saw that Michelle was working the bar.
"You have to serve me, Michelle." Blade called out. She looked at him and then away again. "I'm a club brother, you want me to get you thrown out?"
"Just wait your turn." She said to him. I watched as she served everyone else that came to the bar and left Blade standing there.
"Fuck this." I said as I pulled my hand out from Blade's and walked around the bar.
"What do you think you're doing?" Michelle screamed at me.
"Getting a drink." I said as I pulled a bottle of water and a bottle of beer out of the fridge. I popped the cap off and

handed it to Blade, winking at him.
"You can't just come around here." She said squaring up to me.
"Why not, you weren't serving us, and my man was getting thirsty." I shrugged my shoulders.
"Hey, sweetheart, can you pass me a bottle of Jack." I turned around when I heard Neil's voice. "Heather? What are you doing behind the bar? I don't want you working tonight. I told Dad that."
"Just grabbing a drink as someone..." I nodded my head at Michelle. "Wouldn't serve us." I handed him the bottle of Jack and he leant over the bar and kissed me on the cheek. "Happy birthday, by the way." I smiled.
"Sugar!" Blade called out, my eyes snapped to his and he didn't look happy. He motioned for me to come from around the bar and I did, until I was standing in front of him. "We have to go and show our faces." I nodded and he pulled me close and claimed my lips. I sunk into him, it was never a chore to have to kiss him; I loved every minute of it. I was slowly getting used to living here, it had only been a week but I could see it wasn't too bad.

***

The music was loud, so many people had turned up that the club house doors were wide open and the party had flowed outside too. I was feeling hot and my feet were killing me, I excused myself from Blade who was talking to a group of bikers. I walked outside and found a bench that was empty around the corner from the club house, I needed to sit down. The music was still loud and the men were louder with their shouting at the girls who performed on the stage.
"Hey." I jumped as someone spoke to me. I looked up and saw Mason standing in front of me.
"Hi. I didn't know you was here." I gave him a hug and he held onto me for a bit longer. "Is Daisy here too?"
"Yeah, somewhere. What are you doing out here on your

own? Where's your husband?" He asked as he sat down.
"I needed some fresh air, he's in there somewhere." Mason was my boyfriend from school, I was in love with him and he broke my heart when he joined an MC group at the age of eighteen. He was now named holes as he was a trained piercer. He had a pierced tongue and eyebrow. My mind wandered to what else he had pierced.
"What you thinking?" He asked.
"I was just wandering what else you may have pierced?" I smirked at him. I remember him getting his tongue pierced at the age of sixteen, and the things he done to my body with that piercing was amazing.
"You wanna see?" He asked standing up and popping the button open on his jeans.
"NO!" I shouted. "If Blade comes out and sees that, you're as good as dead." He shrugged his shoulders and continued to undo his jeans. "Please, Mason. Don't."
"I'm hard for you." He said as he grabbed my hand and shoved it in his jeans. He was rock hard and I felt a few piercings too. My body pulsed and I was surprised by how it was reacting. I pulled my hand away and stood up.
"I'm not a club whore!" I sneered at him. "Look at this dress, I'm in red!" I was angry at what he had done and I was also angry at myself for not pulling my hand away sooner and at the way my body reacted to him.
"We have history, Heather. Only a matter of time, you'll want me again." He smiled at me and walked off doing his trousers back up. I watched him as I sat back down.
"What was that? Did you fuck him?" Daisy asked as she walked towards me as Mason walked away.
"No!" I said standing up.
"Why was he doing his jeans up and smiling then?" She pointed over her shoulder and I saw Mason talking to Ryan, Daisy's husband.
"Why is Ryan in green?" I asked, avoiding her question.

"He's on the prowl." She said waving her hand like it wasn't a big deal.
"What are you talking about?" I was confused, did they have an open relationship?
"He's looking for someone to impregnate… I can't have children. We found out last month."
"Oh, Daisy. I'm sorry." I pulled her close to me and held her.
"So, you're looking for a surrogate?"
"No, he's gonna fuck someone, get them pregnant and then we'll have the baby after." She shrugged her shoulders like it was no big deal.
"And you're not bothered that he's gonna stick his dick in another woman?" I asked, shocked that she was so calm about all of this.
"I want a baby, Heather."
"And what if she wants to keep the baby?" I asked, surely it wasn't as easy as that.
"That's not an option."
"Oh, you're having a contract or something?"
"Daisy!" We both looked up and Ryan was calling her over.
"Yeah, or something. I gotta go. Love you." She blew me a kiss as she walked away into the arms of her husband.

***

Blade

I had been talking to the guys from the Bear Devils MC for over an hour, it was a party but business was always talked about. We had to be sure that no one was listening in, so we moved to a corner once Heather had left us for some fresh air. I didn't want to be talking business I wanted to enjoy the party with my girl.
"Look guys, I think we need to discuss this somewhere more private and my heavily pregnant wife is outside somewhere. So I'm going to find her." I shook hands with all three guys

and then went in search of Heather. I found her sitting on the bench, outside, alone.

"Hey, Sugar." I called out as I approached her. She looked up at me and smiled. "You ok?" She nodded and patted the seat next to her. Once I was beside her she pulled my arm over her shoulder and she nuzzled herself into my body. I took full advantage and pulled her as close as I could get her. We didn't speak, it was a comfortable silence until we was interrupted.

"It's cake time." Cammie called out and Heather looked up to her and smiled. I unwound my arms from her, took her hand in mine and we walked back to the club house. We walked in just as Gloria walked out carrying the cake, she was singing happy birthday by herself and once she gave Uno a look he joined in. He gave the other guys a look and they joined in too, that was not something you saw every day, a group of bikers singing happy birthday to a twenty five year old.

"Now, for your present." Uno announced. Everyone including us watched. "Crystal." She nodded her head and walked away, when she returned she had two girls with her, they couldn't have been more than seventeen or eighteen, they were in skimpy outfits and faces full of make-up. "I give you two seventeen year old virgins. Enjoy." He smirked. CG looked appalled, I knew he didn't want to upset his Dad, the Prez of the club. So he grabbed the girls' hands and led them away. Cat calls were called out and the music returned along with the dancers on the stage.

"You wanna dance?" I asked Heather, she looked towards the dance floor and it was full of half-naked women bumping and grinding against the men who wanted them for the night. She shook her head and I pulled her to a booth at the back of the room and we sat down. Roxy approached the table with a tray in her hand.

"You want a drink, sexy?" She asked as she bent over so I could see straight down her top.

"Beer please. Sugar, you want a drink?" She shook her head as she stared daggers at Roxy. I nodded my head at Roxy and she walked off swaying her hips.

"Do you wanna fuck me?" Heather asked out of the blue. I was shocked by her question that I didn't answer her straight away. "Well? I'll take your silence as a no then." She went to stand up and I grabbed her wrist pulling her back down.

"Why are you asking that?" I was confused as hell.

"Answer the question." She demanded. She was being very brave and pushy tonight, if she wasn't eight months pregnant I would have swore she had been drinking.

"Of course I wanna fuck you, you're sexy as hell."

"Then stop looking at her like that." She pointed to Roxy who was now walking back to us, she placed the bottle of beer on the table along with a double whiskey.

"I thought you may enjoy that too." She winked at me. I nodded my head at her and turned my attention back to Heather.

"I am not interested in anyone else." I pulled her close and showed her by devouring her mouth, leaving no room for doubt.

***

The party was in full swing, these things normally went on until sunrise. Though we wouldn't see all of it as Heather was sure to be getting tired soon. She had been quiet for a little while and I looked at her and her focus was on the stage, watching the dancers.

"You ok, Sugar?" I asked her, her head snapped to mine and then back to the stage like she was afraid she was going to miss something.

"Yeah, I'm just watching for some tips." She nodded her head towards the stage.

"Oh, hell no. You're not dancing like that. Just do what you done the other night." I told her.

"I can't keep doing the same routine all the time."

"Yeah you can and then Uno will get bored and pull you off the stage."
"Then how will I pay off the debts? By sleeping around once he's born?" She asked placing her hand on her tummy.
"Ok, fine. But if you wanna keep them interested keep up the routine you done with Cammie."
"Really?" She asked.
"Yeah, guys love girl on girl action." I told her.
"Hmm, is that what you like too?" She asked me.
"I'm not gonna lie, it's great to watch." I smirked at her. "We best get out of here soon."
"Why?" She asked looking around. "It's still packed in here."
"The sex party will start soon. Partner sharing, threesomes, orgies…"
"I get the idea." She said holding her hand up to silence me.
"Come on let's get you to bed. Let me hold you." I said as I stood up and held my hand out for her.
"Wow, cuddling. Score for you." She giggled. We walked past several people, one being the guy from the Cornish Crusaders, the piercer. He looked like he had started the party early, he had a girl riding him, her tits bouncing in his face and he held onto her hips encouraging her to go faster. I noticed that when we passed he stared at Heather and she was looking at him too.
"And you tell me off for looking at other women that way." I chuckled.
"What? No, it was only because they were having sex right there for everyone to watch. I don't think I could do that."
"It happens a lot." I told her as I pushed open my bedroom door and locked it behind me. Heather went into the bathroom to get ready for bed, she had make-up and shit to remove. I pulled off all my clothes apart from my boxers and climbed into bed.
The bathroom door opened ten minutes later and Heather walked out wearing tiny shorts and a t-shirt that was just

covering her bump. I pulled back the covers so she could climb in.
"Thank you." She said shyly. I laid on my back and stretched out my arm offering her a chance to cuddle on my chest, she tried to get as close as possible but her bump was causing us a problem. So she rolled over and I spooned her from behind. Holding her close to my body. It was nice, no awkwardness and what I didn't expect was for her to pull my hand and place it on her tummy, where the baby was kicking. A shot of happiness and sadness coursed through my body, I loved feeling him move. But it brought painful memories of my daughter that was killed. I pushed the emotions and memories to the back of my mind and enjoyed my moment with Heather.
"I'm falling asleep." Heather mumbled. "Give me a goodnight kiss." She demanded. I rolled her onto her back and pressed my lips gently against hers. I was surprised when Heather laced her hands at the back of my head and pulled me closer to her. I licked along her bottom lip until she opened up for me. I found myself hardening and I wanted to climb on top of her and claim her completely. I knew it was too soon and not possible with how big she was now, I wanted to fuck her, claim every inch of her body, but I knew I wouldn't be able to be gentle about it. I pulled away from her and she smiled at me, rolled over onto her side and fell asleep.

Chapter 11

Heather

I woke up to find I was alone in bed, over the last two weeks Blade and I had spent every night cuddled up together and I always woke up to find him snoring. I was beginning to feel like I was happy here, yeah I had to dance a couple nights a week, but I just focus on Blade and pretend that I am dancing just for him. Cammie and I have started dancing together regulary as the guys seemed to really like that. My tummy interrupted my thoughts when a loud growl erupted into the room, I climbed out of bed and quickly showered before I went in search for Blade and food.

The club house was oddly quiet and there was no one in the kitchen, so I made myself some toast and a cup of tea and walked into the bar area to sit down. Cammie was sitting at one of the tables and I walked towards her.

"Morning." I said as I lowered myself onto the chair. Cammie smiled at me and then her attention went back to painting her nails, she huffed and puffed like she was getting annoyed.

"You ok?"

"Yeah." She sighed. "I just can't do this hand." She pointed at her right hand. "In fact, it's all a mess."

"Calm down, let me see." I grabbed her hands and she had made a shocking mess of her nails. I grabbed the nail varnish remover and took all the polish off and started repainting them for her.

"Wow, you're really good at that." She beamed. I smiled up at her as I concentrated on not making a mess.

"Do you want some of these on your nails too?" I asked pointing to a pack of stick on gems.

"They're really fiddly." She told me.
"I think I can manage." I smiled. I had her nails finished within half an hour and she was pleased with the end result.
"Heather, these look amazing. Where did you learn to do that?"
"I'm a trained beautician." I told her. Her head snapped up to look at me, taking her focus off her nails.
"Really? Like you can do the whole waxing and stuff too?" I nodded. "Does Uno know?"
"No, why would he?" I asked.
"He sends us all to a salon in town to get waxed, the guys like us bare. I bet if he knew you could do this that would be a better way to pay off your debts." I liked what she was thinking.
"I'll talk to Blade about it, have you seen him?" I asked, looking around. "Why is it so quiet?"
"Church meeting, a lot of the girls are still in bed... So, can you do my toes for me? Waxing too?"
"I've been asking Blade for the last two weeks to go to my house and get my stuff for the baby, if he lets me I'll bring my equipment with me and then I can do your toes and waxing too." Cammie clapped her hands together and cheered as I said this.
"You've been asking me what?" Blade said behind me. He made me jump and I placed my hand over my heart in an attempt to slow it down.
"To get the baby things from my house." Blade looked at Itch and then back to me. I noticed Itch nod his head slightly.
"Come on then, Sugar. Let's go get them now."
"Really?" I asked and he nodded. I stood up quickly as I didn't want to give him a chance to change his mind. I had to grab hold of the chair next to me as my head swam with dizziness. I tried to focus on the mirror that was hanging on the wall and felt Blade's hands on my waist before I even saw him.

"You ok, Sugar?" He asked me, I smiled at him through the mirror and nodded my head. "You sure?" He looked worried, I knew he cared about me I just wasn't sure how much. I didn't know if we were playing an acting game still or if we were really at the point of being a couple. Did I want that? So soon after James? What Blade and I had was different, he made me feel safe and protected even in this place. When I was in his arms I was calm and collected and I imagined a future together, all three of us. James had always been on the wild side, always out on his bike, drinking and partying. I had met him at a bar when I was twenty and the bad boy side of him called out to me, we were young and reckless and we were married within three months of meeting. I didn't know much about an MC club, James told me he was a brother and they would always come first, that made me feel deflated but I couldn't walk away from him, I had fallen in love with him in an instant. Getting pregnant wasn't an accident, we had talked several times about having a family, when I say talk I mean me trying to convince him it was time to start a family and he kept putting it off, saying he wasn't ready. The day I told him I was pregnant wouldn't be a day that I could forget.

James walked in through the front door with a scowl on his face, he stormed through the house until he reached the kitchen and the first thing he done was pull a beer out of the fridge and emptied the contents in one long gulp.

"Hi." I said quietly not wanting to startle him. "You ok?"

"Club business." This was what he always said when he didn't want to talk about anything. He looked at me and his eyes turned black with desire, I needed to tell him my news before he got distracted. He was always rough with sex and although I normally loved that I didn't want to harm the baby that was growing inside of me. I was still in the very early stages of my pregnancy and I didn't want to risk miscarrying. He stalked towards me and as I was about to speak his mouth came into contact with mine and he was thrusting his tongue against mine. My body responded as it always did, I wrapped

my arms around his neck and he picked me up so I was sitting on the kitchen worktop. His hands ran down my front and under my t-shirt until he had my breasts in his palms, he pulled at my nipples and I moaned into his mouth, moving my body over his hard cock, looking for relief. He released my breasts and pulled at my legs, telling me to wrap them around him. As I did this he carried and slammed me into the closest wall. I let out a yelp and he grinned at me, thinking that I was enjoying this. He turned me around and walked a couple of more paces and slammed me into another wall.
"No, stop, please." I begged. He pulled back and looked at me, confusion written across his face. I took a deep breath. "I'm pregnant." He lowered me to the floor and took a step back.
"How? I thought we talked about this? It's too soon."
"I guess I must have missed a pill." I said shrugging my shoulders, when in fact I hadn't been on my pill for the last six months in the hopes of getting pregnant, but I wasn't about to tell him that.
"You done this." He growled and he pushed me back against the wall, his hand closing around my throat. I tried giving him a pleading look but it wasn't working. "Get rid of it." He demanded.
"NO!" I screamed in his face, pushing at his chest with my hands. He didn't move. "This is our baby, we made this together." He let go of me and began walking towards the front door. "Where are you going?" I called out.
"Out, I can't stand to look at you right now." I slid down the wall until my bum hit the floor and I cried into my hands. I was not getting rid of my baby, if he didn't want it, then I would leave him. I could do this alone.
"Sugar?" Blade's voice snapped me out of my memory and I was glad that I now had him, even though I knew he was keeping things from me, I just hoped in time he would trust me enough to talk about his past.

Chapter 12

Heather

We pulled up to my house in Cornwall in a large truck that Blade had borrowed from the club. I felt a sense of serenity wash over me and I couldn't wait to get inside, I was hoping that Blade would let me stay for a little bit, I missed being in there. As we were about to climb out of the vehicle Blade's phone began ringing. He looked at it and then at me.
"I gotta answer this, stay there, Sugar." He climbed out of the truck as he answered the phone and I watched him pacing up and down, running his hand through his hair, he looked at me every couple of seconds. Once he had stopped moving and had his back to me I climbed out of the truck quietly and started walking towards the front door, digging around in my bag for my keys. I didn't need Blade with me constantly, I was quite capable of going into my house alone and gathering the things I needed. I pulled my keys out of my bag and inserted them into the lock, I turned them and the door didn't unlock. I checked to make sure I was using the correct key and tried again this time pulling at the door handle too. Had someone changed the locks and not told me? I looked behind me to call out for Blade and saw that he had started walking towards me and he looked pissed off. I heard the door behind me open and wondered why someone was in my house.
"Can I help you?" A tall, pretty blonde woman asked.
"Who are you?" I asked. She didn't answer, she opened the door wider and placed her hands on her hips. I looked over her shoulder and noticed that my house had been completely re decorated.
"You come to my house and ask who I am? What do you want lady?"

"Sugar…" Blade said from behind me. I spun around to face him.

"Why is she living in my house?" I asked. "Where is all of my stuff?"

"Oh, has no one told her yet? Awkward." The blonde sung.

"Tell me what?" I stomped my foot as I was getting impatient.

"Well…" The blonde started when Blade interrupted her.

"Thanks, Jess, you can go now." I heard the door behind me shut and Blade held my hand and began leading me back down the path and around the side of the house and towards the garage.

"Where are you taking me? What's going on? Why is she in my house?" I sobbed. Blade stopped walking and wrapped his arms around me until I calmed down. We sat on a garden bench that was near the garage, I don't remember this ever being there.

"Sugar, the Devon MC owns this house." He pointed at my house over his shoulder.

"No, it's mine and James's house, we bought it together nearly six years ago. I had some money left to me when my Gramps died. This is my house now."

Blade shook his head. "I'm sorry, Sugar, all I know is this is one of the Devon MC's properties… All of your stuff is here, in the garage." He got up and opened the large door and I saw all of the baby items and my work stuff too. I needed all of that if I could convince Uno to let me work at the clubhouse.

"Where is all of my money then? If I didn't buy this house?"

"I really don't know." He answered. "Come on, let's grab what you need and load up the truck." He walked towards me and pulled me to my feet. "I'll reverse the truck down here." I nodded and he jogged towards the truck as I walked into the garage.

***

Blade had loaded everything I wanted to take with me into the truck, he refused to let me lift anything except for cuddly toys and bedding.

"Where are we going to put this all?" I asked as we climbed back into the truck.

"We'll make it fit in our room, Sugar." He smiled at me.

"Can we go via the beach please?" I asked, smiling sweetly. He didn't answer straight away so I added; "It's been a shock of a day and I still need answers, I'm guessing I'm gonna have to speak to Uno about that. I just want to breathe in some fresh Cornish sea, please?" I pleaded, placing my hands on his arm. He nodded and I squealed in excitement.

A few minutes later we were pulling up to the beach at Portwrinkle, the sky was blue with only a small scattering of clouds. The sound of the sea relaxed me instantly and I couldn't wait to paddle in it. I was thankful that I wore a summer dress and sandals today. I climbed out of the truck and looked at Blade.

"You're not really dressed for the beach." He was wearing a black t-shirt and jeans. Biker boots and his leather cut, telling everyone he was part of the Devon Destroyers MC. "Lose the boots and jacket and roll up your jeans." I told him as I slipped my feet out of my sandals. He stood there staring at me. "What?" I asked. He strolled towards me and pressed me up against the truck.

"I'm the one that tells you what to do, not the other way around, Sugar." He growled as he trailed kisses and nibbles down my neck.

"Blade…" I panted, he knew exactly what buttons to push to make my body feel alive. I was craving the intimacy and soon I wasn't going to be able to wait much longer.

"This will be the one and only time I do as you say, got it?" I nodded and he placed a chaste kiss on my lips before he proceeded to remove his boots and leather cut, leaving them in the truck.

We walked hand in hand down the steps and across the pebbly beach towards the sea.

"Ow, fuck. Why did I have to remove my boots to walk across stones that hurt my feet?" Blade complained.
"They're pebbles and it's the beach experience. Come on." I tugged at his hand and we walked closer and closer towards the sea, I breathed in the salty sea air, I missed this so much. Living in Devon wasn't the same as Cornwall, if I got the choice in the future I would definitely move back here.

Blade

It was a whole different experience watching Heather on the beach, she had a constant smile on her face and her light brown, wavy hair blew in the warm breeze. She stood in the sea and her feet sunk into the wet sand. She giggled and wiggled her toes and the sea washed up over her ankles.
"Come and stand next to me." She called out, looking over her shoulder at me.
"No, thanks." I said, waving my hand at her.
"Please?" She pouted and I couldn't resist that look. I found myself walking into the freezing cold sea and standing next to her.
"Fuck, it's freezing." I complained hopping from one foot to the other.
"Your body will adjust to it, stop complaining. Now, stand in the sea and let your feet sink into the sand, when the waves come up over your feet you'll feel like you're moving." I done as she said just to humour her, I really didn't see how the sea covering my feet would feel like I was moving. She placed her hand in mine as the waves edged closer and closer to us.
"Ready?" She asked, looking at me with a huge smile on her face. I nodded and edged my body closer to hers, I wanted to claim her lips. She had never looked sexier to me, the smile and light in her eyes did things to my body. As I leaned towards her the sea came up over my feet and my head dizzied and I did in fact feel like I was moving, so much in

fact I fell onto my ass right in the sea. Heather let out a yelp as I must have splashed her and as she looked down at me she burst out laughing, holding onto her expanding tummy. I looked up and saw another wave heading for us, I scrambled to my feet quickly and ran across the beach. Heather walked towards me slowly, her hips swaying and the smile on her face was my undoing, I plowed towards her and crushed my lips to hers. After a couple of seconds, she pulled away, slightly.

"You taste salty, like the sea." She giggled, our lips still touching as she spoke.

"Hmm and I wonder why that is?" I chuckled. "Come on." I pulled at her hands ready to get back to the truck.

"Can we go for a little walk first?" She asked.

"Sugar, I'm soaking wet and I'm sure I've got sand all around my balls." I said as I adjusted myself in my wet jeans.

"Take your jeans off, your boxers will dry in the sun as we walk."

"There's just one problem with that." She looked at me eyebrows raised, waiting for me to continue. "I'm not wearing any boxers."

"What are you wearing then? Briefs?" She asked, looking confused as she knew I only wore boxers.

"Nothing on under here, Sugar."

"Oh." She said, her eyes widening in surprise. "Let's get back then so you can get into some dry clothes." I nodded and we walked hand in hand back to the truck, I held her door open for her as she climbed in. She reached behind her and grabbed one of the baby towels and began drying her feet so she could slip her sandals back on. I opened my door and began undoing my jeans.

"Oh my God, what are you doing?" She shrieked.

"Taking off my wet jeans, I can't drive home in these." I explained and I began pushing them down, she threw the towel at me and I manage to catch it before it landed on the

sandy ground.
"At least cover yourself up so you won't be done with indecent exposure." I chuckled as she blushed and looked away. I covered my cock with the small towel and I lowered my jeans and jumped into the truck. I pulled the towel away to dry my feet so I could get my boots on. She glanced at me and her head quickly snapped back around as she saw that I was exposed.
"Ohmygod." She said it like it was one word. "This isn't how I thought I'd see your cock for the first time." I smirked at her.
"Oh really? So you've thought about seeing my cock, have you?"
"What?" She squeaked, looking back at me but keeping her eyes fixed on mine. "Yes, no! Umm…"
I chuckled throwing my head back against the headrest on the seat. "It's ok, Sugar. Let's get home." Once I had my boots on, I placed the towel over my semi erect cock, it wasn't that I was turned on, it was just how Heather made me feel, constantly. She breathed a sigh of relief and her shoulders softened once I was covered up again. I grabbed her hand and kissed the back of it, laying it high on my thigh, I expected her to pull it away but she left it there, torturing me all the way home.

Chapter 13

Heather

We walked into the clubhouse together, I was eager to talk to Uno about my money and what I thought was my house and Blade needed a shower and some clean clothes before he started unloading the truck. I walked in ahead of Blade and the bar area was full of bikers and the sweet buns. They all stopped to look at us and then a chorus of laughter broke out as everyone saw that Blade was trying to hide his manhood under a tiny blue towel.

"What the fuck happened to you?" Itch asked as he got up and walked towards us.

"We went to the beach and he fell in the sea." I told him.

"You." Itch pointed at Blade. "On the beach and in the sea? That I would have paid to see." Itch laughed.

"Heather wanted to go to the beach while we were in Cornwall. I gotta keep my woman happy." He shrugged his shoulders.

"I bet she's keeping you happy in plenty of ways." Itch winked at Blade and they high fived each other. I turned to scowl at Blade and he had already began to walk away. I looked around for Uno and I couldn't see him.

"Where's Uno?" I asked Itch, he shrugged his shoulders and walked away. I saw Neil sitting at a table in the back of the room with his laptop and I made my way over towards him. He should know where his Dad was. "Hey, am I interrupting?"

He shook his head and kicked the chair opposite him out with his foot, he did this a lot. He was tapping away on the keys and I didn't want to disturb him. I don't know how he saw the keys as the club house was dark and he was also sat in a dark corner.

"What's up, Heather?" He asked, still not looking away from his laptop.

"I need to speak to Uno. Do you know where he is?" He shook his head and pulled out his phone from his pocket, he tapped on it a few times.

"He'll be here in a min." He said, concentrating back on his computer. He was quiet and not talkative, which was not like him at all.

"Are you ok?" I asked, leaning closer towards him, resting my elbows on the table.

"Yep." He clearly didn't want to talk to me, so I stood up and went to walk away when I bumped into Uno.

"Oh, hi." I said quietly.

"You wanted to see me? I'm used to women chasing after me, but I didn't think you would ever be one." He smirked at me, looking me up and down which made my skin crawl.

"I need to ask you a couple of questions." I told him.

"Well, you can ask, I may or may not answer." He sat down next to Neil and pulled out a cigarette and lit it.

"Dad, come on, she's pregnant." Neil said, nodding his head towards me.

"It never done you any harm." He replied not putting his cigarette out. "If she don't like it, she can talk to me later." I didn't want to waste any more time, I needed answers. I sat back down at the table and tried not to cough or breathe too much when Uno blew his smoke towards me. "Well, sweetheart? Spit it out."

"I went to my house today and there was someone else living there…" I paused.

"Yeah, it's our house." He stated.

"I was under the impression that James and I had bought it, I gave him a lot of money. Where is that money, if the house is yours?"

"You see, sweetheart." Uno said leaning on the table that separated us. "James had a bit of a problem." I looked at him confused, I didn't have any idea what he was talking about.
"He liked to gamble, pay the girls at 'Skins' a visit, you know lap dances and other stuff…" He waved his hand in the air.
"Dad." Neil said in a tone that was warning him not to say too much.
"So, where's my money?" I could feel myself getting upset and emotional, my gramps had left me that money and I was happy that I was putting it towards something useful and now Uno is telling me that James gambled it away.
"It's all gone, sweetheart. We paid his debts once the money was gone, why do you think you're here?" I shook my head, not believing what he said to me, all the money was gone. My gramps worked hard for that money and it was all wasted on gambling and girls. My heart was racing in my chest, I was upset and angry. James was never the person I thought he was, he had always stayed that young rebel that I fell in love with. No woman or baby was ever going to be enough, he sure put on a good enough act to make me believe he wanted me and our son. A sob rose up and out of my throat and I stood up quickly, not wanting to cry in front of them. I ignored the fact that my head spun and I walked away quickly, exiting from the club room and heading towards Blade's bedroom, I needed to lie down. I had tears running down my cheeks and my vision was blurred so I stopped and leant against the cold, hard wall and focused on my breathing. I felt a few sharp pains low in my tummy which made my breath catch in my throat. Something didn't feel right.
"Sugar?" Blade called out as he came rushing towards me. "What's happened?"
"It's gone. It's all gone." I sobbed again. He didn't answer so I knew he assumed I was talking about the money. "I need to lie down." I said, all of a sudden feeling exhausted and weak.
"Come on." He helped me stand up straighter and I cried out

in pain, clutching low on my tummy where the pain had hit.
"Sugar?"
"Something doesn't feel right." I looked at Blade and his face was full of worry.
"Are you in labour? Shit, we need to get you to the hospital."
"My water hasn't broke so I don't know what it is. I just have this pain." I placed my hand low on my tummy again, showing him where it was. He nodded and cradled me in his arms and rushed towards my car. He placed me in the passenger seat.
"Fuck, where are the keys?" He shouted. I dug around in my bag until I found them, handing them to him.
"Blade, you need to calm down. Everything will be ok." I tried to calm him, though in fact I had no idea why I was getting this pain and I wasn't due for another four weeks. I rubbed my hand over my tummy, praying that my little boy was going to be ok and that he was still safe and healthy.

***

Blade

I rushed Heather into the hospital explaining that she was pregnant and having pains but that she wasn't due for another month. They got her into a room quickly and checked her over. They checked the baby's heartbeat first and that was strong and healthy, we were now waiting on an ultrasound scan. I was pacing around Heathers room, if his heartbeat was good that meant he was healthy, but I didn't understand why Heather had been getting pains. A nurse wheeled a large machine into the room and began setting it up.
"Are we ready… Dad?" My head snapped up to look at her, was she calling me Dad? I looked at her and then looked at Heather, she smiled at me and held her hand out for me. I had to tell them she was my wife so they let me come back into the room with her. I walked towards Heather and held onto her

hand as the nurse squirted some gel onto her tummy and ran a wand over it.

"Here we are, baby looks good." The nurse began explaining everything and I zoned out, not listening, I was just thankful that Heather and the baby were ok. "It's false labour I'm afraid. I'll get your discharge papers." The nurse left the room and I looked to see Heather looking calmer.

"Hey, you zoned out, what were you thinking?" She asked me. I shook my head and placed my hand on her tummy and kissed her lips.

"I'm just glad you're both ok."

About thirty minutes later Heather was discharged and we were making our way back to the club house. As we walked in Cammie came running towards us.

"Oh my God, are you ok?"

"She's fine. She needs to rest." I told her as we carried on walking towards my room. Once I had her inside I made her lie down so she was comfortable. The doctor said not to overdo it and to relax as much as she can. I lay beside her and ran my fingers through her hair, she was getting sleepy.

Bang. Bang. Bang. Heather jumped and I swore under my breath.

"Prez wants to see you, man." Riz called out from the other side of the door.

"Fuck." I cursed as I climbed off the bed, I looked back towards Heather and saw she was getting up too. "Where do you think you're going?"

"I'm gonna get some of the baby stuff from the truck." She said as she slipped her feet into her sandals.

"Like hell you are. You need to rest. Now, back on the bed." I demanded. She didn't move, she stood staring at me. "Now!" I growled. She sat back on the bed with her back to me.

"Sugar…" I tried to say calmly.

"Just go, the Prez wants you." She didn't look at me and I knew it was because she was angry with me, for telling her what to do. If she wanted to survive in this world, she needed to realise what the bikers say, goes.

I walked out of the bedroom and into the bar area, I scanned the area looking for the two prospects.

"Wayne." I called out and once his head snapped up to look at me, I nodded for him to come closer. I looked around again until I saw Dwayne, his twin brother. These guys hadn't been prospecting with us for long but they seemed to have a lot of potential. Once they both stopped in front of me, I passed them the keys to the truck and told them to unload everything and drop it all off at my room.

"Knock first, my Old Lady is in there." I told them.

"Sure thing, Blade." Wayne said and then they disappeared off outside.

"Blade!" Uno shouted from behind me. Shit, now he was going to be pissed that he had to ask for me twice. I made my way towards him and we walked into his office. "Sit." He demanded. I did so without saying a word.

"I need you down at 'Skins' tonight…"

"Prez, my woman has just got back from the hospital, false labour. I don't wanna leave her." I said cutting him off. He paused in his movements and glared at me.

"You'll go where I need you." He told me. I shook my head, I couldn't believe I was back in this club, being told where I had to go and what I had to do. "You understand?"

"Yeah."

"Take Riz and CG with you… I need CG to access the computers, check the cameras are all still working."

"What are we looking for, Prez?"

"We had one girl OD last week, according to everyone she never took drugs. Which meant someone forced them on her."

"Drugs?" I asked. Uno nodded and he was talking as I stared into space.

"Baby, wake up. Please, wake up." I began shaking her and she wasn't moving, her eyes were wide open and staring into

space. I placed my hand on her bump and there was no movement, my little girl always responded to my touch. I looked up from my crouched down position on the floor and looked up at the guys who had surrounded me.

"We found her here." Riz said, placing his hand on my shoulder. We were in the grounds of the Devon Destroyers MC.

"We need an ambulance!" I shouted.

"No." Prez stepped forward looking at me. "She's gone, they both are." I stood up and faced him.

"My baby could still be alive." I growled.

"Oh, God." We heard a whimper behind us and I saw Gloria, the Prez's wife at Willow's side. She had pulled her t-shirt over her bump and what we saw was a message.

"Blade." Prez said, nudging me with his foot on my chair. I looked up to him and nodded. I would not let what happened to Willow happen to anyone else. "Your girl is needed on stage tonight, too."

"No, no fucking way. She's been in hospital today." I growled as I stood up, placed my hands on his desk and leant forward. "This whole debt thing is a pile of shit and we both know it. You knew I'd want her and you saw it as a way to get me back in the club. No dancing, not tonight." I pushed away from the desk and stormed back out to the bar to grab a drink.

"Hey, handsome." Michelle purred at me.

"Shut it and get me a whiskey." I growled. I didn't want anything to do with her, I wanted to calm my raging heart and the hurt that had come with that memory. The only way to do it was by drinking.

***

Riz, CG and I walked into 'Skins'. It was dark, except for the bright spot light that was covering the stage. Currently there was a girl on the stage with long blonde hair.

"I'm heading to the office." CG said as he walked away.

"I'm going to find Beauty, the brunette that I saw last week." Riz said. As he went to walk away I grabbed the back of his jacket.

"We're here to work, not for fun." I told him.
"We need to get friendly with the girls, for information." He winked and strolled away. I had only been in this place a couple of times before. I knew that the girls had stations they worked. Some of them worked the stage, others were waitresses, there were lap dancing girls and back room girls. Those were the girls who earnt the most money and got to keep all of their tips. Brittany, the girl who was found OD'd was a back room girl.
I walked around, familiarising myself with the layout of the place and who was working where. I kept my eyes on the clients and tried to seek out anyone who looked dodgy. CG was making sure the cameras were covering all the girls, Prez had decided to get some new ones installed last night and CG was making sure they worked.
After being in the club for a few hours, nothing looked suspicious. I headed towards the office to check on CG, I hadn't seen Riz since we arrived. I didn't bother knocking and just walked straight in. The last thing I expected to see was CG with a girl spread out on the desk and him feasting on her. She wasn't dressed like the other girls and I realised it was because it was Tiffany, she was in charge of the girls hair and make-up, she was a behind the scenes girl.
"Ahem." I cleared my throat and CG looked up at me.
"Shit, fuck." He growled as he stood up and pulled Tiffany's skirt back down into position, so she wasn't exposed. He held onto her hand and helped her off the desk and she blushed when she saw me. "Get back to work." He told her and she nodded her head and walked away, quickly.
"Having fun working?" I chuckled. CG cleared his throat and swung his chair around to face the monitors.
"All the cameras are set up, I have one on each of the back rooms as that's where Brittany worked." I nodded and scanned the screens, my eyes stopped on one screen.
"Do these things zoom in?" I asked.

"Yeah, see something you like?" He chuckled.
"Fuck off and zoom in on this one." CG zoomed in and I swore.
"What? What is it?"
"That's a Satan." I pointed to the guy who was banging a girl from behind and pulling her head back with her hair.
"How do you know?" He asked me.
"The tattoo on his right shoulder, I've seen that enough times to know who they are… Get him the fuck out."
I heard CG pick up the phone. "Security, I need the man in room five escorted out. He's never to be let back in here."
"Wait, get them to hold him. I want a word with him." He nodded and told the security guys to wait out by the back door with him. I got up and moved towards the door, with CG hot on my heels.
"What are you going to do?" He asked.
"I want information." I growled. "I've dealt with these guys enough to know how they work." As I opened the door to the office I almost plowed straight into Riz, he had a shit eating grin on his face.
"How was Beauty?" CG chuckled.
"As good as always, I wish I could convince her to come to the club."
"Get a lot of info?" I asked.
"Nothing concrete." He replied. I shook my head and pushed past him, Riz wasn't interested in helping; he was only interested in getting his dick wet from a different chick than a club whore. I rushed down the stairs and out the back door, where two large security guys had a hold of the man I recognised.
"Thanks, guys." I said, they nodded and headed back inside.
"Look who we've got here." I said as I walked around this guy in a circle while CG and Riz stood back to watch.
"What the fuck you want, man?"
"What are you doing here? On our turf? This is Devon MC

property." I growled.
"Is it?" He smiled. "Didn't know." I grabbed him by the throat and pushed him into the brick wall with a force so hard that I heard his back crunch.
"You been in here feeding our girls drugs?" I growled in his face. He didn't answer, he only smirked. I was about to ask more questions when I heard a rumble of bikes and gun shots.
"Blade, get down." Riz shouted. I looked towards them as they fell to the floor and took cover behind some large bins. The bikes were headed towards us and they were firing, I used this guy as a shield until I could get to cover. Once I was close enough to hide behind the security van, I let go of the guy and he fell to the floor, not moving.
"Fuck." I cursed and pulled my gun out of my jacket. I looked towards Riz and he was in the same position as me. We both counted to three and began firing back, which caused the bikers to retreat. Once it was quiet we all stepped out from our cover and I looked over to the guy I had been questioning earlier and he had been shot dead.
"Who were they? I didn't get a good enough look." Riz asked, walking towards me. I was stood over the body.
"I'm guessing they were coming for their buddy over here. CG you got cameras out here?"
"Yeah, I'll go and look."
"We need the info fast, leave Tiffany alone this time." I told him. I wasn't any more important than these guys, but I had dealt with the Satan MC before and knew we had to act fast. They would be seeking revenge on losing a brother and soon.
"I'll call the clean-up crew." Riz said as he was dialling his phone. I nodded and followed CG into the club.

Chapter 14

Blade

"Fuck!" Prez yelled as he stood up and began pacing the room. We had called a church meeting as soon as we got back. CG had pulled up the recordings from the outside cameras and we discovered it was in fact the Satan MC. "We need to keep a close eye on these guys. I want all the 'Skins' girls here, today. Gather them all up. They're not safe there. I'm calling a lockdown for all the women. Get your Old Ladies and families here."

"I'll gather their addresses and shit." CG said as he began tapping away on his laptop. That thing was practically attached to him.

"I want everyone here, this is not a drill. I don't trust these guys." Prez said.

"So we closing 'Skins'?" Ripped, the VP asked.

"No, we'll still open like normal but there will be some of you going with them every night." We all nodded and Prez slammed the gavel down, indicating that the meeting was over. We all climbed to our feet and I went in search of Heather. I hadn't seen her for hours and I was hoping that she was still ok. I scanned the bar area and I couldn't see her, Cammie was on stage dancing. I made my way to the backstage area to see if Prez was making Heather dance. The room was empty so I made my way to our bedroom. I walked in and Heather had been busy, all the baby stuff was set up. Furniture had been moved so there was room for the changing table and moses basket. If she had been moving furniture I was going to spank that gorgeous ass of hers. I walked towards the bed and saw that Heather was asleep, I brushed her hair out of her face and looked down at her. She was peaceful and I didn't want to wake her. I stood up and made my way into the bathroom for a much needed shower.

Heather

I woke up when my baby boy kicked, I smiled to myself and then sat up as he was pressing on my bladder and I needed the toilet. I stood up and walked towards the bathroom and that was when I heard Blade in the shower.

"Blade." I called out. I waited and he didn't answer. "Blade." I called out again, knocking on the door this time.

"Yeah?" He called back.

"I need the toilet." I called as the baby moved and I thought I was going to wet myself.

"I can't hear you. Just come in." He called back. I pushed the door open and kept my eyes focused on the floor. "You ok, Sugar?"

"I really need the toilet." I told him.

"Go ahead." My head snapped up to look at him and he had shampoo in his hair and it was falling down his body along with the water. "Sugar?" I looked at him again and nodded. I walked quickly to the toilet to relieve myself. One thing I never thought I'd be doing is peeing in front of him. I couldn't help but watch him in the shower, the muscles in his back as he leant forward in the water and rinsed his hair. I walked over to the sink and watched him in the mirror as I turned on the tap to wash my hands.

"Aaahh." I turned around when I heard the noise from Blade, he was staring at me with the shower door open. "Sugar, did you just turn on that tap?" I nodded and then realised that by me turning on the hot water tap it must have taken it away from the shower.

"I'm sorry." He was now standing fully naked in front of me and I focused on not letting my eyes wander over his body. I reached for the towel that was laying on the wash basket and passed it to him. He chuckled as he wrapped it around his waist, not bothering to dry the rest of his body. He grabbed my hand and led me back to bed.

"The room looks good, but if I find out you moved this furniture, I'll be spanking that ass of yours." He growled the last bit. The thought of it alone made my body seem like it was on fire and I found I was already craving his touch. I wanted to know what it would feel like to have his hands and mouth on me, everywhere. My breathing picked up and soon I felt like I was panting.

"Sugar, you ok?" Blade asked as he pulled back the covers so I could climb in. I nodded and got myself comfy, laying on my side so I could face him when he got in. I watched him as he lost the towel and climbed straight in. He normally wore boxers to bed. He faced me and I placed my hand on his bicep, the one that had the tattoo of the tree on it.

"Who's Willow and Lily?" I asked as I traced my finger over his tattoo. His eyes darkened immediately and he slammed his lips onto mine. My body temperature instantly grew and he was kissing me with urgency, intensity and I was loving every minute. I hooked my leg over his and pulled it closer to me, trapping it between my thighs. His hands were moving over my body and he left a blazing trail where his fingertips touched. My body was pulsing and I needed a release, it had been too long.

"Blade." I moaned.

"Kade." He said and my eyes popped open to look at him.

"It's my name, Sugar. Call me Kade." I nodded and he trailed kisses down my neck.

"Please." I begged. I rolled onto my back and Blade held his head up with his hand, leaning on his elbow. He placed his hand on my large bump and I moved it down until it was above my mound. "Please, touch me." I begged, again.

"You sure?" I nodded as I bit my bottom lip. He kissed me

softly as his hand disappeared into my bed shorts. As soon as his finger touched my clit I jumped, it was sensitive and I needed to come. He pushed my shorts off and I kicked them off my feet. I moaned in the back of my throat and arched my back as much as I could. I remembered that he was naked, when he pushed his fingers inside of me I grabbed the back of his neck and pulled his lips close to mine. While he was distracted I let my hand run down his body until I had his hard cock in my hand. I began to pump him and I heard him groan into my mouth, as his fingers fucked me he thrust into my hand.

"I need you to fuck me, Kade." He shook his head.

"Not tonight. The doctor said not to overdo it and I'm sure this is overdoing it." He smirked.

"Faster then. Please, make me come." I moaned. He lowered his head and gently nibbled on my nipple through my vest top. I cried out and I felt his pre cum coat my hand, I used it to help with the movements. I felt a tingling start low in my back and my legs began to shake, I could feel my release coming.

"Come on, Sugar. Give it to me." He pressed his thumb into my clit and bit my nipple and the sensations over took my body and I was calling out his name. A few seconds later I felt his release shoot over my tummy, which was now bare as my vest top had slid up over my large bump. My chest was heaving up and down, I was trying to calm my breathing down when I felt the bed move and Blade walked into the bathroom. He came back with a cloth to wipe me clean. After he was finished I pulled my vest top off over my head, I wanted skin to skin contact with him. He climbed back into bed and pulled me up against him, kissing the back of my neck. Within seconds he was fast asleep.

Chapter 15

Heather

We had been on what Blade called 'lockdown' for a couple of weeks, it meant that we weren't allowed to venture outside by ourselves and there were a lot more girls here at the club house. Blade said they were the dancers from 'skins' and that they needed protecting too, he wouldn't tell me from what, I got the usual 'It's club business'. I knew better than to argue with it. The Old Ladies and kids were brought here too, for safety, so the usual partying and sex had been restricted to certain rooms.

"Hey, Heather." Cammie called out as she walked into the room that was now my beauty room. Uno had agreed to let me set up my equipment, it meant that the girls didn't need to go out to get their waxing done anymore.

"Hey, you ok?" I asked her. She nodded and began undressing so I could do her waxing treatment.

"I need it bare." She told me and I got to work.

***

"Wow, that didn't hurt as much as normal." She told me, as she sat up and reached for her clothes.

"Yo, sweetheart." Ripped called out as he walked into the room.

"Hey, you can't just walk in here." I complained as I stood in front of Cammie to block her from being seen. He looked over my shoulder and smiled.

"I've seen it all before." He chuckled. I went to speak again when Cammie cut me off.

"Heather, it's fine. We can't be shy when we are sweet buns."

Cammie walked around me, only wearing a vest top, she stood on her tiptoes and pulled the VP's head closer to her and devoured his lips, I heard him growl and he picked her up so she could wrap her legs around his waist. He moved towards my massage couch and I stood in front of it.

"No, you're not doing it here." I placed my hands on my hips and he broke apart from Cammie's kiss. "Besides, she's just been waxed, she should wait for the redness to calm down."

"Get. The. Fuck. Out." He demanded. I looked at Cammie and she nodded her head at me. I quickly walked out of the room and in my haste I bumped into someone.

"Oh, sorry." I said as I looked up to see a small, dark haired girl stood in front of me, she looked like she wasn't more than twenty.

"No, it's all my fault. I was too busy looking at this thing." She pointed towards her phone. "I'm looking for Neil."

"Neil?" I asked. I had never heard anyone else call him that, apart from me. Then it dawned on me, was I not supposed to call him that? Blade had asked me to call him Kade, but it felt strange in front of everyone else, so I saved it for when we were alone.

"Oh, sorry. CG. I'm Tiffany. I work at 'skins', I do the girls hair and make-up."

"Oh, hi. I'm Heather, I… Well… Blade is my… I'm his…"

"Old Lady." Blade's voice said from behind me as I hesitated. I spun around to look at him and he was smiling at me. "Hi, Tiffany."

"Hi, Blade. It was nice meeting you, Heather." She walked away and Blade prowled towards me.

"What was with the hesitation?" He asked as he wrapped his arms around me.

"Well, we've never actually… Um… It was all for show, in the beginning." I stumbled on my words.

"You're my Old Lady, got that?" He said as his lips hovered above mine. I could feel the warmth from his breath and my eyes closed in anticipation of his kiss. I nodded and as he moved to kiss me the door to the salon opened. We both moved our heads to see Cammie and the VP coming out. I looked at Cammie and she had tears in her eyes.

"Are you ok?" I asked her, breaking away from Blade and grabbing her hand. She nodded and wiped at her eyes, smearing her mascara over her face. "What did you do to her?" I screamed at Ripped, facing him.

"Blade you better get your woman out of my face before I remove her myself." He growled.

"Sugar..." Blade said in a warning tone.

"No, he's hurt her."

"I'm fine, I promise." Cammie said to me and I turned back towards her.

"You need better control over that woman of yours." Ripped said as he walked past us all.

"Sugar." I looked at him over my shoulder, not bothering to turn around. I wanted to make sure Cammie really was ok.

"You can't talk to another brother like that, especially the VP."

"But..."

"No! As my Old Lady, you come above the sweet buns and the 'skins' girls. But never above a brother." I nodded to let him know that I understood what he had said. He moved towards me and I turned around to face him. He kissed me softly and then walked away.

"Come on." I pushed the door open and walked inside, followed by Cammie. "Sit down and tell me what happened."

"Honestly, I'm fine." She said as I started making a cup of tea. I held up the mug to offer her a drink. "Coffee please... Heather, I'm ok. I promise."

"You had tears in your eyes." I said. She looked towards her hands that were folded in her lap.

"He likes to choke me." She started to explain and I turned around so fast to look at her that I nearly fell over.

"What!" I screamed.

“It increases the pleasure, he cuts off my air supply… Not fully, I can still breathe. It just makes my eyes water.” She shrugged her shoulders and I handed her a mug full of hot coffee and sat down beside her.
“Why are you here? Why do you let them do this to you?”
“I love this world, bikes and bikers are hot. I thought being an Old Lady would be great…” She paused and took a sip of her drink. “I needed a place to go, I had nowhere to stay. After…”
Knock. Knock. Knock.
“Oh, sorry.” I said to her. “COME IN!” I called out. I was surprised when Bump walked in, smirking.
“I want a massage.” He demanded. I stood up and looked around for the quickest way to escape, I wanted to tell him no and tell him to fuck off, but Blade’s words came back to me ‘you come above the sweet buns and the ‘skins’ girls. But never above a brother’. Would I have to do as he says, massage him? I felt myself start to tremble, I was scared to be alone in a room with him after the last time.
“She’s about to do my waxing, VP said it needs doing asap.” Cammie said as she got to her feet and stood in front of me.
“Fine, I’ll be back in a couple hours.” He turned around and walked out the door, as soon as it was just me and Cammie again I breathed a sigh of relief.
“Thank you.” I said as I squeezed her hand.
“No worries, let’s shut this place up and get some lunch. Just make sure you stick with Blade for the afternoon, he won’t let Bump near you.” I nodded and we both walked out of the salon room, looking to make sure Bump wasn’t anywhere around. The coast was clear so we made our way towards the kitchen.

Chapter 16

Blade

Heather and I were sitting on the sofa, the TV was on and we were relaxed and chilled out. My hand was on her bump and the little boy inside was kicking.

"Brothers." Prez called out, I looked up and he nodded his head.

"I'll be right back, Sugar." I kissed her on the forehead and strolled over to where they were all standing.

"We're having a party. Those bastards aren't ruining all our fun. 'Skins' can stay shut, the girls can work here..."

"What about the kids?" CG asked.

"We'll keep all adult partying to the pool room until the little kids are in bed. The slightly older ones will be living this life soon, let them see what goes on, it didn't do you any harm." He chuckled.

"You had me at these parties from the age of thirteen..." CG said.

"What are you complaining for, you lost your virginity when you were fourteen, a lot of kids would kill for that and with an older, experienced woman." He winked at CG and slapped him on the bank.

"I lost my virginity to a club whore, I'd never let that happen to a son of mine." He growled and walked away.

"CG, YOU GET BACK HERE!" Prez shouted. CG stopped walking, looked over his shoulder and shook his head, like he was disappointed in Uno. "GLORIA, go and sort that bloody kid out." She looked at him and nodded. "Now, there will be a party. We'll have extra prospects on the gate, let's have some fucking fun." We all cheered in agreement and the plans for the party were in full swing.

***

Heather

The party had started over an hour ago, there was a few small kids running around, so the entertainment hadn't started yet. I was surprised that I hadn't been told to dance, but then the 'skins' girls were here and they were more experienced and sexier than me. I was looking for Cammie as I wanted to carry on our conversation that got interrupted earlier. I walked around the corner and saw her sitting at the bar, I walked towards her and sat on the stool next to her. She was talking to Michelle and I didn't want to interrupt

"He has a thing for her, he's never slept with the sweet buns." Cammie told Michelle. I wondered who they were talking about, I was about to ask when Michelle said;

"What about those two virgins on his birthday?"

"He never slept with them, I saw them when I was out shopping last week. They were complaining that they wanted to be with a biker and when they got one they said he was a 'pussy' and wouldn't fuck them." They were talking about CG, so who was the girl they were talking about that he had a thing for? Michelle placed a bottle of water in front of me and I smiled at her, we had never got on, she wanted Blade and he wanted me, so she hated me.

"Hi, Heather." I looked beside me to see that Tiffany was sitting on the stool next to me.

"Hi, Tiffany. You ok?" She nodded and started looking around. "You looking for someone?"

"Yeah, Neil. Oh, um... Yeah, CG. Have you seen him?" I shook my head.

"You want a drink?" Michelle asked her.

"Just a coke please." Michelle raised her eyebrows in surprise and poured her a coke.

"Don't you drink?" Michelle asked her as she placed the drink on the bar in front of her. Tiffany shook her head as she took a

sip and then spit it out.
"What's in that?" Tiffany yelled.
"Just a bit of vodka." Michelle chuckled. Tiffany covered her mouth and ran away crying. I went to move off the stall to follow her when I felt Blade's hands on my hips.
"Where are you going?" He whispered in my ear.
"I just want to check on Tiffany..."
"I'm sure CG will be keeping her occupied soon." He chuckled. "The kids have all gone to bed, come and watch the show with me." I nodded and he spun me around and slammed his mouth onto mine. I gripped the front of his t-shirt in my fists and opened my mouth so our tongues could connect. I felt the familiar buzz go to my clit, my body now knew how he could make me feel. He still hadn't fucked me, but I could feel his determination fade every time he made me orgasm.
"Let's sit over here." He grabbed my hand and led me towards a booth that was at the back of the room, in a dark corner.
"What's the show?" I asked as he pulled me in beside him.
"You'll see." He winked at me as Roxy approached our table.
"Can I get you a drink, handsome?" She smiled at him.
"Grab me a couple of beers and some water for Heather, then don't interrupt us again." She nodded and walked away.
"I haven't seen Neil all night, have you?"
"Sugar, did he ask you to call him that?" Blade asked as he placed his arm over my shoulders.
"I can't remember, should I not call him by his name?"
"Call him CG, that's his club name." I nodded and we were silent while Michelle delivered our drinks.
"It's starting." Blade whispered to me. I looked towards the stage and there were a couple of girls stood in only their underwear and heels, they started dancing and grinding against each other. I looked around the room and the guys were all focused on the stage, some had girls with them,

pleasuring them as they watched. Was this what Blade wanted me to do? Was that why we were in a dark corner. "Stop thinking and watch the show." He whispered to me. I looked back towards the stage and both girls were now naked, they were stroking each other and kissing.

"Are we watching a sex show?" I hissed at Blade.

"Just watch, Sugar." He said without his eyes leaving the stage. Was this what he liked? Did he want a threesome? Oh, who am I kidding, I bet he's already had them. I watched as the girls paid special attention to each other and soon enough one was bringing the other one to orgasm. It was hot watching it, hearing the sounds of panting and cries of pleasure. My body felt like it was on fire and I squirmed in my seat, I definitely needed to be fucked. I turned towards Blade and he was watching me.

"You wanna get out of here?" He asked, I nodded frantically and he pulled me up from my seat. We walked quickly across the room and had to stop when Bump stepped out in front of us. The sight of him was enough to turn my body cold.

"I want a massage." He said, looking at me. I looked up at Blade and he was staring at Bump.

"You do not go anywhere near my woman." He growled.

"She's offering a service and I want that service." He demanded.

"It's not that kind of massage." I added.

"Did you just talk back to me?" He shouted, I shrank back in fear and tried to hide behind Blade.

"She's mine and not massaging you, ever. Got it?" Blade told him.

"Yeah, you've said you've claimed her but I don't see a patch on her. That makes her fair game." He smirked, taking a step towards me. Blade didn't hesitate and threw a punch at him. I yelped and took a step back. A few seconds later they were in a full fight, punches were being thrown and bottles and tables had been pushed to the floor. I looked around and saw that

the club members were all watching and cheering them on. I ran towards Riz.
"Please, stop them. Break it up." I pleaded.
"Calm down, sweetheart." He wasn't going to help so I moved onto the next member pleading with them all and no one would break it up. All of a sudden it went quiet, I looked around and saw that Bump was out cold on the floor and Blade stormed towards me, picked me up and carried me away.

Blade

I pushed the door open to our room and carried Heather inside, I placed her on the bed and took a step back. I couldn't believe the nerve of Bump, wanting my woman. Everyone knew from the start, as soon as she arrived here that I had claimed her.
" Are you ok? You're bleeding." Heather said as she stood up and stepped towards me.
"Yeah, I'm fine." I turned around and walked towards my wardrobe, I pulled the door open and chuckled as the majority of clothes in there belonged to Heather. I grabbed what I was looking for and walked back towards her. "Sugar, I'm going to need you to wear this." I handed her the leather vest.
"What is this? Why?" She turned it over and read what it said on the back. "Property of Blade. Devon Destroyers MC. Property?" She asked, eyebrows raised.
"Sugar, it's a vest the Old Ladies wear so the other guys know that you are taken. Will you wear it? Be my Old Lady?" She held it in her hands and looked at it again. She stood up and slipped it on.
"How does it look?" She asked, turning around so I could see my name on her.
"Fucking hot." I pulled her close and kissed the hell out of her, until I bruised her lips and she would still feel me when we

pulled apart. My cock also loved her in that jacket and I wanted her in only that. I groaned at my thought and Heather pulled back.

"Are you ok? Did Bump hurt you?" She placed her hand on the side of my face and I laughed out loud.

"That piece of shit couldn't hurt me if he tried. He's a pussy." I stepped back and shrugged out of my leather cut and placed it on the back of the chair. I pulled my t-shirt off over my head and I watched as Heather's breathing changed. She couldn't take her eyes off me. I took a step closer to her and she immediately reached out to place her hands on my naked, tattooed chest. "Let's get cleaned up." She nodded and I led her towards the bathroom. I turned on the shower as she reached in the cupboard for some towels. As the water heated I pushed her new leather vest off her shoulders and let it fall to the floor, closely followed by her t-shirt and jeans. She pulled her bottom lip into her mouth and looked at the floor, I pushed her chin up with my finger so she had to look at me.

"You're beautiful." She smiled shyly at me, tied her hair up so it was on top of her head and removed her bra and underwear. I quickly stripped out of my jeans and boxers and held her hand as we climbed in the cubicle shower. It was a tight fit, but it only meant I had to be that much closer to her. I pulled her back against my chest and as the water pounded onto our skin I kissed and nibbled at her neck.

"Mmm, Kade, that feels nice." She moaned and I felt my cock jump, my name coming from her lips was sexy as hell. I couldn't wait until she was screaming it. I leaned forward and grabbed the shower gel, I washed her body from head to toe and she insisted on doing the same to me, though she spent a lot of time washing my chest and cock. By the time we were both clean, I was ready to get her dirty again. We climbed out of the shower and I wrapped a towel around Heather and she released her hair from the tie and it bounced down over her shoulders and down her back. I had images of me behind her,

with a fist full of hair.
"Umm, Kade?" I looked at her and she giggled. "Shall we do something about that?" She pointed to my cock that was now standing tall and proud.
"And what do you suggest, Sugar?"
"I have an idea." She winked at me and walked out of the bathroom, I followed her out and she dropped the towel and climbed onto the bed on all fours. Her pussy was pointing directly at me and I had to do everything I could not to climb up behind her and slam into her.
"Lie on your back, Sugar." I told her and once she was in position, I hovered above her, making sure not to press into her baby bump. I kissed her lips and trailed kisses down her neck, stopping at her nipples to lick and nibble them. She moaned in pleasure, arching her back which spurred me on and I moved over to the next one to give it the same attention. I was satisfied when she was squirming on the bed. I wanted her wet, I wanted to tease her, I wanted to hear her begging me.
"Kade." She sighed. I loved hearing my name falling from her lips in pleasure. I continued down her body until I could smell and taste her arousal, I flicked my tongue over her clit and she cried out and let her legs fall apart on the bed. I feasted on her until she cried out again, running my tongue all the way up through her folds, I could taste her sweetness and knew that she was becoming my new addiction. My cock was painfully hard and I wanted to be inside of her.
"Please, Kade, I need more." She begged as she palmed her breasts in her hands. I grabbed her hips and pulled her to the edge of the bed. I was on my knees and I couldn't wait any longer, I rubbed my cock over her, she cried out every time I hit her clit and then I pushed into her slowly. "Wait!" She called out. I stopped moving and looked from where we joined to her face. She was sitting up, leaning on her elbows. "We need a condom." She told me.

"Sugar, you're already pregnant." I chuckled. She moved back until I slipped out of her, my balls were aching and I needed to be inside of her.

"I don't know how many people you've been with, how many whores. I don't want to catch anything." She explained.

"Sugar, I'm clean. I promise." I told her, she shook her head.

"No condom, no sex." She told me. I groaned as I climbed to my feet and rifled through my bedside table until I found protection. I picked it up and showed it to her, she smiled at me and laid back down on her back. She scooted back to the edge of the bed and let her legs fall open. The sight of her wet, swollen pussy had me almost coming on the spot, I quickly covered myself and got back down onto my knees, lined myself up and pushed inside of her, slowly. She was hot, wet and tight. I could feel her throbbing around me and I needed to move before this was all over too quickly. I moved in and out of her slowly, I didn't want to hurt her and I was conscious of the fact that she only had a few weeks left until the little guy would grace us with his presence.

"Please, Kade, faster, harder." She moaned and pleaded. I sped up but I wasn't going to pound into her like I really wanted to. I pushed her legs further open and pulled her ass up so I could go deeper, she called out and I felt her tense and her walls throbbed and squeezed me, tight. I increased my pace and looked up at her, her hands were fisted into the bed sheet and her chest was rising and falling. She called out my name and I carried on until my release erupted through my body. We were both breathless and I pulled out of her and disposed of the condom before climbing back on the bed with her.

"You ok, Sugar?" I asked as I kissed her gently on the lips, her eyes were closed and I wasn't sure if she had fallen asleep. She nodded her head and when she opened her eyes they were watery. "Shit, did I hurt you?"

"No. I'm sorry, it's just hormones." She said as she waved her hand over her bump. I chuckled and told her to move up the bed so we could climb under the covers.

Heather

I felt happy and relaxed laying in Blade's arms. I had my back to his chest and we were both still naked. The release was so intense that it made me cry, the worried look on Blade's face wasn't a look I wanted to see again. I felt a major connection between us and I wanted to know more about him, I didn't actually know anything. If he had any family, where he was from, he was practically a stranger.

"Kade?" I asked, his breathing was deep and I wasn't sure if he had fallen asleep.

"Hmm." He barely answered.

"Willow, was she your wife?" I asked. He didn't answer straight away but I felt his hands moving; one trailed over my bump and to my clit, I knew what he was doing he was distracting me with pleasure and although I wanted to fight it, my body betrayed me and responded to him. I pushed my ass back into his hard cock and wiggled. I felt him move away and then I heard the rustling of a condom wrapper, I smiled to myself as I knew what that meant. He rolled back towards me, he held my leg up in the air slightly and pushed inside of me. I groaned and he pulled back and pushed inside just a little harder.

"Yes!" I cried out.

"Hold your leg up." He demanded. I grabbed my leg and he pulled and pinched my clit. I cried out again and I could feel my orgasm approaching, my leg was shaking and I couldn't hold it up. I let it fall and I moved so Blade slipped out of me. He looked at me and I kissed him as I climbed onto all fours.

"Please, fuck me. You won't hurt me. Please?" I saw his eyes darken and he nodded, climbing up the bed so he was positioned behind me. He slammed into me and I cried out, it felt so good and I wanted and needed more. I pushed back against him, trying to feel him deeper. His hands firmly gripped my hips and he started a punishing rhythm, my arms started shaking so I lowered the front half of my body onto the bed. A few seconds later, Blade grabbed a fist full of my hair and yanked me up, I cried out as it hurt but felt good at the same time.

"Come on, Sugar. Come for me." He growled. He pulled on my hair every time he pounded into me and I was screaming and calling out his name. A couple more thrusts and Blade was coming with me as another orgasm coursed through my body. He released my hair and I fell onto my forearms, trying to get my breathing to even out. "Fuck, that was amazing, Sugar." Blade growled as he pulled out of my body, I turned myself so I could flop onto my back, my chest was rising and falling quickly. I had never been fucked so amazingly in my life. Now, I'd had him, no one else would ever measure up. He would be my new addiction.

Chapter 17

Heather

"Kade, I need to get my waxing done. The baby is going to be here in a couple of weeks. Please?" I begged.

"Why can't one of the other girls do it? Tiffany, she does hair and make-up." He said. He didn't want me leaving the club house and I still didn't know why. No one even knew who I was, and no one would know I had anything to do with the Devon MC.

"It's not the same, babe. I need a professional. Wouldn't you like me to be all bare down there?" His eyes lit up and I knew I had him.

"Fine. I'm coming with you." He told me, I nodded and as we were about to walk out of the room there was a bang on the door.

"Church." Riz yelled out.

"Fuck. Can you wait an hour?" He asked me.

"It's only open for another hour, I need to go now." He nodded and dragged me out of our room. We walked into the clubhouse and Blade looked like he was looking for someone.

"Wayne." He called out and a younger lad walked towards us. He had on a leather jacket that had the Devon MC logo on it and Prospect was on it too.

"What you need, Blade?" He asked and then smiled at me.

"My Old Lady needs to go into town. You take her, stay with her. Leave your jacket behind, then no one should recognise you. Keep her close and if anything happens to her, you're responsible." Wayne nodded and Blade turned towards me and pulled me close for a kiss. "Do what you need to and come straight back." I nodded and he walked away.

"Let's go." I said as I walked towards the clubhouse door. It was a lovely sunny day and all I really wanted to do was go and sit on a beach. I climbed behind the wheel of my car and Wayne looked at me. "What?"
"Maybe I should drive." He said.
"I can drive perfectly fine, thank you very much. Now get in, before I leave without you." He scrambled around the car and jumped in. I wouldn't have really left without him, Blade would kill me.
"So, where are we going?" Wayne asked as I headed towards town.
"Sammy's salon." I told him. "What the fuck are you doing? It says fifty not twenty." I screamed at the driver in front of me that was crawling along at a snails pace.
"You having your hair done?" He asked.
"No, waxing. Oh, seriously you're just gonna pull out in front of me!" I shouted, blasting my horn at the same time.
"Heather, we aren't meant to be drawing attention to ourselves." Wayne reminded me.
"Oh, shit. Sorry. I get a bit of road rage." I said shrugging my shoulders. I pulled up outside the salon, turned the car off and went to get out.
"Let me check to make sure it's safe first." Wayne said, stopping me from getting out. He pulled off his jacket and tucked his gun into his jeans and covered it over with his t-shirt. "Wait here." I nodded and he got out of the car and walked around to my side, he was constantly looking around and eventually he opened my door and quickly got me into the salon.

Blade

"You let her go out?" Prez roared, standing up.
"Wayne's with her." I said shrugging my shoulders. "You've let the 'skins' girls go home. Nothing has happened."

"You of all people know what the Satan MC are like, they will want revenge for that guy you used as a shield." He roared.
"He shouldn't have been on our turf in the first place. He got what he deserved." I said playing with the blade of the knife that I had in my hands.
"Get her back here. NOW!" He roared and everyone around us was deadly quiet.
"I'll call the prospect." I told him as I stood up from the table to where it was quieter. After I had spoken to Wayne, I re-joined the table as the Prez was saying;
"VP, Riz and Bump. You are on duty tonight at 'skins'."
"Sure thing, Prez." Bump said.
"My pleasure." Riz smiled. He had a thing for Beauty that worked there, which surprised me as I always thought he had a thing for Cammie; she was always the girl he went to first.
"Blade, you know where the Satan MC compound is, take some prospects and see what you can find out. Send one in if you have to." Prez said.
"What are you wanting us to find out?" I asked.
"What the fuck they're up to. I don't like surprises. That's all." He slammed the gavel down. "CG wait for a minute."
The rest of us got up and walked out. Before I left Prez said;
"Blade, get that girl back here. If that baby gets harmed, you're taking responsibility. Now, get out." He slammed the door in my face and I found myself wondering why he wanted Heather's baby to be ok? Since when did he care about her? Something wasn't right and I needed to find out what was going on.

Heather

"I may just have my nails done too, while I'm here." I said to Stacy, the beautician.
"No, we need to go." Wayne said. I looked at him. "Blade called, we need to get back." I nodded and sighed, it would

have been nice for someone else to do my nails for a change. I paid for the treatments I had done and we walked out of the salon.

"I think I'll drive back." Wayne told me, taking the keys from my hand. He shut my door once I was seated in the passenger side and as I was about to put my seat belt on I heard the screeching of tyres and a bang. I looked up and saw that a motorbike had crashed, I jumped out of the car.

"Call an ambulance." I shouted to Wayne as I walked past him as quick as I could to get to the bike.

"Heather, no!" Wayne shouted as he grabbed hold of the top of my arm. "That could be anyone."

"That's a Cornish Crusader patch. It could be my brother in law." I told him. He shook his head.

"I can't let you go. We need to get back to the clubhouse. Other people are helping him." I looked over my shoulder to see other people surrounding the bike and one person looked like they were about to remove his helmet.

"Let me go." I said, trying to pull my arm away.

"Sorry, sweetheart. Not happening." He began to drag me back towards the car and I pretended I was in pain, I cried out and held my tummy. As his grip loosened I hit him in the balls and ran as good as I could towards the biker.

"NO!" I called. "Don't remove his helmet, he could have a head injury." I knelt down on the floor beside the bike and flipped the visor up. I don't know why but I was expecting to see my brother in law, Ryan. I didn't expect to see bright blue eyes staring back at me. "Mason? Shit, are you ok?"

"Yeah, it's just my leg that hurts. Can you pull my helmet off?"

"No, not until the ambulance is here, just in case. Do you have a headache?" I was trying to think back to all the first aid training that I had done. If he had a concussion I needed to keep him talking, he couldn't go to sleep, though he seemed with it and not dazed at all.

"No, seriously, babe. I'm fine." He smiled and held hold of my hand. I felt relieved that he wasn't seriously hurt. I felt someone's hand around my arm and I looked up to see Wayne standing over me.
"We need to go."
"No, I'm not leaving him. If Blade doesn't like it, then it's tough." I heard the ambulance siren and then everything happened so fast, Mason was put on a stretcher and we were both ushered into the ambulance and were speeding away before I knew it. I heard Wayne swearing and saw him running for my car. I didn't intend to get into the ambulance with Mason, I guess as I was holding his hand they assumed we were together. Blade was going to be mad when Wayne called him.
"Your husband will be fine." The paramedic said to me and before I had a chance to correct him, we had pulled up to the hospital and Mason was taken inside and to an examination room. I was told to wait in reception and I didn't like the idea of being there by myself, what if someone had been watching us and now I was alone. I moved to a seat where I could watch the main door and the door where they took the emergency patients through.
It felt like I had been waiting ages and I was starting to feel tired. My eyes were closing when I heard;
"Sugar!" My eyes snapped open and I saw Blade heading towards me. I stood up, expecting him to shout at me for not staying with Wayne but he pulled me in close to his body and held onto me tightly.
"I'm sorry, I didn't expect to be bundled into the ambulance too. I just wanted to keep Mason company." I breathed in his scent and my body came to life and my appetite for him was in full swing.
"We contacted the Cornish MC, they are on their way. We can go home." I nodded. I wanted to see if Mason was ok, but I knew that Blade was only wanting to keep me safe. I would

contact Daisy in a few days and check up on him.

***

Blade

Heather and I had just climbed into bed after she danced on stage with Cammie, doing their double act. I still didn't like it but I was not the Prez of this club, if I was things would be a lot different.

"So, did you get it done?" I asked her.

"My waxing? Yeah, if you had joined me in the shower you would have seen."

"If I had joined you in the shower, I would have fucked you up against it." I growled at her as my cock came to life.

"Hmm, that would have been nice." She moaned. I placed my hand on her face and kissed her. She moved my hand down her body until it was between her legs. We had given up wearing clothing to bed. She was smooth and wet, and I needed to have a taste. I rolled her onto her back and made my way down her body and used my tongue on her smooth silky folds until she was screaming.

We laid facing each other, Heather was trying to get her breath back. She leaned towards me and kissed me on the lips. She trailed her hand down my chest and to my shoulder, she pushed me flat on my back and climbed on top of me. She rubbed her sweet, wet pussy over my cock, her tits were bouncing and she looked sexy as fuck.

"Sugar, you're killing me here." I groaned. She looked over at the bedside table and nodded her head towards the condoms. I reached out to grab one and handed it to her. She ripped it open with her teeth and moved slightly so she had the room to cover me. Once she was satisfied it was on correctly, she lifted her body and impaled herself onto me.

"Fuck!" I called out as I wasn't expecting that. It felt amazing. I had hold of Heather's hips, keeping her steady as she worked her way to a release on my cock. I nearly lost it a

couple of times, but I held on until she was ready. "Come for me, Sugar." I demanded.
"Shit, I need the toilet." She called out as she climbed off me and ran into the bathroom. A couple of minutes later she walked back towards the bed. "I'm sorry, it must be the baby pressing against my bladder."
"It's ok, climb back up here." I told her, my cock was still fully erect and I needed to feel her warmth surrounding me. She climbed back onto the bed and straddled me, she leant forwards and ran her tongue over my bottom lip, I growled as she was teasing me. I pulled at her nipples and palmed her breasts, she pushed them into my hands and rose higher above me, I pulled a nipple into my mouth and sucked hard, she cried out and I let my hands trail down her body, I wanted to make sure she was ready for me. I let my fingers trail over the inside of her thighs and over her smooth folds. She adjusted her hips so my fingers slipped and were against her clit, she moved her body as I kept my hand still, she worked herself over my hand and I could tell she was getting closer. I moved my hands and clamped them onto her hips and I helped her position herself over the top of me. She slowly sat down onto me and I felt her walls tightening almost immediately. She stayed sitting up straight and ground her body onto mine. I thrust my hips up into her a couple of times and she cried out. She leant back placing her feet onto the bed and her hands were holding onto my legs for support. She began moving her body up and down, it was sexy as hell as I could see myself disappearing into her. I began flicking her clit and she suddenly sat up.
"I need the toilet again." She went to climb off me and I grabbed onto her hips, keeping her in place.
"Sugar, you just went. Go with it, trust me?" She nodded and I started moving my hips up into her body. She placed her hands onto my chest and began riding me harder and faster.
"That's it, just let go."

"Kade…" She panted. Her body moving out of control, she could feel her orgasm approaching as she was trying to force it out of her body. I pressed my fingers onto her clit, she stopped moving and cried out as I emptied myself into her.
"Oh my God, I wet myself." She sobbed. "I told you I needed the toilet." She went to climb off and I held her still.
"Sugar, you didn't wet yourself, you came. You squirted over me."
"I… What?"
"You female ejaculated… Have you never done that before?" She shook her head, looking down at our bodies where they were connected. "How did it feel?"
"Amazing, I've never come so hard… I thought I'd wet myself." I smiled up at her.
"I think we need another shower." I laughed, she nodded and climbed off me. We walked into the bathroom to clean ourselves up before climbing into bed for the rest of the night.

Chapter 18

Blade

All we seemed to be having recently was church meetings, it seemed like we had one every day, sometimes a couple a day. Over the last couple of nights, I had been scoping out the Satan MC compound, they were only situated an hour away from us. I took Wayne and Dwayne with me, we kept note on what they were doing and who was coming and going.

"Tell us what you found out." Prez said from the head of the table.

"Not a lot, nothing seems to happen over there. A few bikes come and go, but that's about it."

"They have to be plotting something." Prez shouted. "You need to tell us what went down after you found Willow, when you went enforcer, to get revenge." I looked around the table and everyone was staring at me, waiting for me to talk.

I didn't have a plan, I didn't know what I was going to do. All I knew was that I needed revenge. The Satan MC had grabbed my six month pregnant wife, fed her drugs until she OD'd, killing my baby girl too. Then dumped her body back at my MC compound, with a nasty looking 'S' carved into her tummy. Our club and theirs had a few fallings out in the past, they claimed we were working their turf, with the drugs we shipped. We were only the carriers, we didn't sell it ourselves, it brought in a good profit. The area we worked hadn't been claimed by us or them so we saw it as neutral ground, they didn't see it the same way.

I had been camped outside of the Satan MC for days now, trying to find a way in, I couldn't just walk up to them as they knew my face. I saw an opportunity arise and I went for it, not thinking twice about it. I followed one of the Old Ladies into town, she was alone and didn't have a prospect with her. The thing about MC clubs is the women were the most treasured things to them, especially the Old Ladies. I watched as she shopped, not a worry or a care in the world. I didn't want to hurt her, I wasn't that sort of person, but I did need revenge for what they had done to Willow and Lily.

I waited until she climbed back into her car, then followed her, once it started to get dark I rode up behind her car and started flashing my lights. I could see her looking in her rear view mirror and she started to slow down. I couldn't believe my luck was in, was this going to be that easy? Once she had stopped the car I pulled up my bike beside her and pulled out my knife.

"You scream or try and run, I'll gut you like a fish. Got it?" She whimpered and nodded her head. "Move to the passenger side." She slid over onto the other side of the car and I got off my bike and climbed in. I drove to the Satan MC compound and the prospects let us through the gates without taking a second look at us, if that had happened at the Devon MC someone would have been in serious trouble.

"Is there a back entrance to this place?" I growled. She nodded and pointed to what looked like a fire door, there was a prospect guarding it. "Are there guards everywhere?" She nodded. I stopped the car and got a good look at her, she must have been in her early twenties, she had long black hair and pale skin. When I looked at the leather vest she was wearing I saw that she was the VP's Old Lady. I grabbed the top of her arm and dragged her out of the car, knife still in my hand, ready to use if I needed to. We walked to the back door and when the prospect turned around he saw me, he reached for his gun and I drove the knife right into his neck, hitting a major artery. He fell to the floor, spluttering and struggling to breathe. I stepped over him, dragging the woman with me, we walked in through the door and I looked around.

"What's your name?" I asked her, looking around corners and making sure no one was about.

"Libby." She whispered. I nodded and came to a halt when the main club room came into view, it was crowded and I didn't want to be spotted.

"Where's the Prez's office?" I asked.
"At the back, down that hall." She pointed. I nodded and walked towards it, being careful not to be spotted. When we reached the door I listened to see if I could hear anyone, a couple of voices were inside but I didn't know who it was.
"Knock on the door. I'm going to stand here, don't try and warn them." She nodded, tears running down her face. She wiped her face and raised her hand to the door, knocking loudly.
"COME IN!" Someone shouted. That had to be the Prez. She looked at me and I grabbed her again, from behind and held the knife to her throat.
"Open the door." I told her. I watched as her shaking hand reached out for the door handle. She pushed it open and I stormed in holding her. There were only two guys in the room. "Nobody move!" I shouted as I pushed Libby further into the room.
"I'm sorry, Prez, VP. I was out shopping when…"
"Enough!" Bellowed Prez. "Nice to see you, Blade." He smirked at me. I pushed Libby into a chair and stood beside her the knife still threatening her. "What can we do for you?"
"I want to know why you did it? She was innocent in all of this, why kill my wife and baby?"
He laughed out loud throwing his head back, he walked around his wooden desk and leant on it so he was closer to me, I kept my eye on the VP too. He was looking at Libby, but he didn't look concerned for her.
"Why are you wearing that?" He asked her. She stayed quiet and looked at the ground.
"It was a good message we sent, wasn't it?" He smirked.
"Fuck this, I'm outta here." The VP said as he walked towards the door.
"No one leaves, else I'll kill her." I really hoped they didn't think I was bluffing, I didn't want to have to kill her but I could stab her so she looked injured but wouldn't be critical, unless they let her bleed to death. The VP wouldn't let his Old Lady bleed to death, would he?
The VP and Prez both laughed at the same time and before I knew

what had happened the VP had drawn his gun and shot her, she slumped over in the chair and I threw my knife that lodged in his throat. I pulled my gun out of the back of my jeans and pointed it at the Prez.

"Don't even think about moving." He held his hands up in surrender. "Why would he shoot his Old Lady?"

"Libby is a club whore. I don't know where she got that jacket." He shrugged his shoulders.

"Now tell me, why did you do it? Why her?" I yelled as I stormed towards him and held the gun against his temple.

"She was an easy target." He smirked. "We had been watching your house, you never kept a prospect with her. She didn't fight when we grabbed her, when we forced her to the floor and injected her with heroin, over and over again." He laughed.

Bang. Bang.

I didn't hesitate, I pulled the trigger and he fell to the floor. I thought I would have felt a sense of relief knowing that I had got my revenge, but I still felt as empty and hollow inside. I didn't know how I was going to go on without my girls.

"How did you get out of there?" Riz asked.

"I pulled on the VP's jacket, grabbed a bike and rode out of there. Left the bike and jacket on the side of the road, when I picked up my bike." I shrugged my shoulders.

"And no one knew you were there?" Prez asked.

"I didn't see anyone, unless there were cameras in his office."

"I can hack into the system and check that." CG said as he began typing away.

"So, we assume that the only reason they may be out for us is because of the guy they killed, that Blade here used as a shield."

"It's gotta be, Prez." I said.

"Hold up." CG said not taking his eyes off the computer. "No cameras in the Prez's office, though I've checked through the other cameras and the club house looks deserted." We all looked at each other; that was strange. It's not like a club to just up and leave.

Beep. Beep. Beep. Beep.
"Fuck, that's the front gate alarm. A prospect is down. Everyone get out, Riz secure the girls." Prez shouted and my first thought was Heather.

Heather

Cammie and I were having lunch with Michelle and Tiffany. I thought it was strange how the other 'skins' girls went home but Tiffany didn't.
"So, Tiff. How come you're still here?" I asked as I took a sip of orange juice.
"Um... CG asked me to stay?" She said it like she was asking a question. We all stopped eating and looked at her.
"You his Old Lady?" Michelle asked. Tiffany shook her head. I was about to question her more when all of a sudden the guys came rushing out of the meeting room, guns drawn and looking around. I searched for Blade and once our eyes met I calmed slightly. Until I heard the sound of Bikes and guns going off.
"Ladies, move, now. Chelle, take them to the secured room." Riz said, she nodded and we all stood up.
"Everybody down!" Ripped yelled as bullets came firing into the club house. Cammie pushed me behind the bar and I fell down so hard I cried out, clutching onto my stomach.
"You ok?" She asked. I nodded. We were under attack for some reason and I didn't want to complain about the pain I had in my tummy. All I was concerned about was not getting shot and hoping that Blade was ok. The sound of guns firing felt like it went on for ages. I felt a large pain shoot through my tummy and I cried out.
"Cammie!"
"You ok?" She asked, crawling towards me on the floor.
"What's all this water back here? Fuck, has your water broke?" I nodded as tears streamed down my face. "It's ok,

you'll be ok. I just need to find Blade." She went to move and I grabbed hold of her hand.
"Please, don't leave me." I begged.
"What's going on?" Michelle asked.
"Heather's in labour. We need Blade." Cammie told her. She nodded her head.
"I'll go find him." She said. It had gone quiet and I didn't want to cry out in pain. Just as Michelle had stepped out from behind the bar, we heard Ripped shout;
"Michelle, get down." Another round of gun firing started and Michelle was hit, she fell to the floor where we could see her. All three of us screamed and Tiffany crawled towards her to see if she was alive. She looked back at us and shook her head. A sob rose from my throat and I felt scared. I hadn't felt this scared when I was told I would be living with a group of MC guys. I was scared that Blade would be taken from me and scared that I might have to deliver my baby behind the bar in a MC club house.

***

"Cammie?" I whispered. It had gone quiet and the pain was increasing. I hadn't heard the guys in a while, so I didn't have a clue what was going on.
"You ok?" I shook my head.
"I need to push."
"Oh no." Tiffany squeaked.
"It's ok, we can do this." Cammie said to me. She reached up to the bar and pulled down a pile of clean bar towels and laid them on the floor. "I need to remove your underwear so I can have a look." I nodded. "Yep, I think I can see the head. When you get the urge to push, just go with it." I nodded.
"How do you know about this?" I asked, panting through the pain.
"I had a baby."
"I need to push." I told her and I used all of my strength to push until I couldn't anymore.

"Tiffany, come and hold her hand, Heather breathe. Then push again, he's not moving."
"What. Happened. To. Your. Baby?" I asked fighting through the pain. "I need to push again."
I pushed with all of my strength, squeezing Tiffany's hand so hard that I thought it was going to break.
"He's coming, keep going. Yes, that's his head out. One more big push. Come on, Heather." I was exhausted but found the strength from somewhere. As soon as I heard him cry I sagged in relief. I looked up and Cammie had him wrapped in a bar towel and she passed him to me. Tears streaming down her face too.
"I need something to secure the cord with."
"Here, use this." Tiffany said as she pulled a couple of hair grips out of her hair. Cammie secured and cut the umbilical cord.
"Thank you. Thank you so much." I appreciated Cammie so much, but now she meant even more to me. "What happened to your baby?"
"He was still born."
"Oh God." I sobbed covering my mouth with my hand. She waved her hand in the air as if to dismiss the conversation.
"We need to get you to the hospital." Cammie said as she looked up and over the bar.
"No!" I called out. "You can't go out there, look what happened to Michelle."
"It's all quiet now. I'll be fine." She said crawling to the end of the bar. "I can see Riz." She waved her hand. A few seconds later she crawled back to us. "He waved me back and told me to be quiet." She whispered.

Cammie

Thirty minutes later and Heather was looking really tired, her eyes were heavy, she was pale and she looked like she was

finding it difficult to hold her baby boy as he fed.
"Heather." I said shaking her. "Wake up."
"No, tired. Can you take him?" She asked quietly. Once the baby pulled away from Heather I held him in my arms and tried to wind him. I looked down at the floor and then up at Tiffany.
"Is that all her blood?" She asked.
"Yes, she really needs to get to a hospital. That can't be good." I looked at Heather again and she had fallen asleep.
"Heather." I shook her and she wouldn't wake up. "Shit. Here, take the baby. I have to get help." Tiffany nodded. I crawled to the end of the bar again and saw that Riz was sitting in the same place. I crawled quietly over to him, avoiding all the broken glass and debris that had been damaged. He was gesturing for me to go back and I shook my head. Once I reached him, I whispered; "Heather had the baby, she's bleeding, a lot. She needs to get to the hospital, now!"
"Fuck!" He swore.
"Where's Blade?" He shrugged his shoulders and told me to get back to safety. I crawled back to behind the bar, Heather looked awfully white. I checked her arm for a pulse, it was there but very faint. She had lost too much blood. I tried several times to wake her but it was no good. I heard doors opening and footsteps running, I was praying it was someone coming to help.
"Sugar?" I looked up and saw Blade looking down at us.
"Fuck!" He roared, causing the baby to cry. His eyes snapped to the bundle in Tiffany's arms and he softened.
"Blade, she needs to get to the hospital, now. Her pulse is very faint. She's lost lots of blood."
"Fuck, the nearest hospital is an hour away." He said as he bent down and picked her up.
"Drive fast, brother." CG said as he slapped Blade on the back. I ran to get the baby's car seat. We were soon settled in the car

and speeding away to the hospital. Blade broke every speed limit and we made it to Knightsbridge hospital in under forty minutes.

Chapter 19

Blade

Cammie ran into the hospital and got help and soon enough a couple of doctors were pulling a trolley out to get Heather on.
"What happened?" One of the doctors asked.
"She went into early labour, delivered the baby at home. We couldn't stop the bleeding." Cammie informed them as I pulled Heather out of the car and laid her on the trolley. They pushed her inside as another doctor came and took the baby, to get him checked out.
"Does he have a name?" The female doctor asked as we followed them through the crowds of people waiting to be seen.
"No." I said, regretting not asking Heather what she wanted to call him, in case she didn't make it through. We followed all of the doctors until we came to a door. One of the nurses stopped and turned towards us.
"You need to wait here, while the doctors work on her."
"Where has she gone?" Cammie asked.
"Straight to surgery, to try and stop the bleeding. There is a family room over there if you want to wait in the quiet."
"Thank you." Cammie said.
"What about my son?" I asked. My son? Shit, where had that come from?
"He's just being checked over. As long as he's ok; you'll have him back before you know it." I nodded at her and Cammie dragged me to the waiting room.
We walked in and it was empty, there was a coffee machine by the window and I needed something to calm me down. Cammie sat in one of the chairs staring at the door.

"Coffee?" I asked. She shook her head, she was twisting her hands constantly together in her lap and she wouldn't take her eyes off the door. I stood and looked out of the window, praying that they would both be ok. Cammie had said that Heather had fed the baby and that he seemed healthy. Which made me feel slightly better. The door opened and a nurse walked in with a clipboard.
"Mr. King?"
"Yes." I said as I stepped towards her.
"Your wife is bleeding very heavily still, as she is unconscious we need your consent to do an emergency hysterectomy."
"Oh no." Cammie sobbed.
"What's that?" I asked. The nurse explained everything and I signed the forms and sent her on her way. "She won't be able to have any more children?" I asked Cammie.
"No, she'll have her womb removed." I gave the consent they needed to be able to save her life, I just didn't know how she was going to react to it after having I done.

***

We had been sitting in the family room for over an hour when the door opened again and a nurse walked in carrying Heather's son.
"Mr. King?" I nodded and she walked towards me. She was carrying him in her arm and had the car seat in the other one.
"I understand your wife is still in surgery?" I nodded. "I brought this so you can feed him." She handed me the baby and the bottle. "Do you need help?"
"No, my sister has a child. I've had plenty of practice." I sat down in the chair, cradled the boy in my arm and began feeding him his bottle as the nurse told us all of the tests that he'd had done. He was fit and healthy and could go home with me. "Thank you." The nurse smiled at both of us and left the room. Cammie looked at him as I fed him.
"He's so handsome." She smiled.

"Thank you for delivering him." She smiled again and squeezed my leg with her hand.

***

After another three hours the door to the room opened and a doctor walked in. Cammie had the baby in her arms, trying to get him to sleep. I stood up and walked towards the doctor, Cammie followed me.

"Mr. King?" I nodded. "We have finally managed to stop the bleeding, I'm not going to lie, it was tough. She lost a lot of blood and now she's in recovery…"

"Is she going to be ok?" I asked, cutting him off. "The boy needs his Mum."

"We're just waiting for her to wake up, she's in intensive care on a ventilator…"

"What's the recovery time? How long will she have to stay in here?" I asked.

"We'll have to wait until she wakes up. She'll be in a lot of pain, she won't be able to drive, do any housework or anything strenuous for about eight weeks, minimum. She should be ok to leave the hospital after about four or five days."

"Can we see her?" Cammie asked.

"One at a time and the baby can't go in there. Once she is conscious, she'll be moved to another room."

"Thank you." I said, grabbing the doctor's hand and shaking it. "Thank you for saving her." He nodded his head, smiled and left the room. I was relieved that she was going to be ok.

"Knock, knock." Said a female voice, I looked around and saw Tiffany and CG standing in the doorway.

"What are you doing here?" I asked.

"We thought you might need this." CG said holding up a baby changing bag.

"Oh, yes. We do, thank you." Cammie said, grabbing the bag and walking through the door that was connected to the

room. It was a toilet, but it also had a baby changing table in it.
"How is she?" Tiffany asked. I explained to them everything the doctor had said, running my hands over my short hair several times. I felt relieved that she was going to be ok, but I wouldn't relax until I saw her brown eyes and heard her sexy voice.

Chapter 20

Blade

The doctor had been in and told us that they had removed the tube from Heather's throat as she was waking up. I was sitting in the chair beside her bed, clutching hold of her hand tightly, willing her to open her eyes. A few minutes later she started moving and her eyes fluttered open and then closed again. I stood up, leaning over her and placing my hand on her cheek.
"Sugar? You awake?" I whispered. She was still in the recovery room and there was also a couple of other people in here too. I didn't want to disturb anyone. Her eyes fluttered again and I stroked my fingers over her cheek. I finally saw what I had wished for, her gorgeous brown eyes staring at me. I smiled at her and she placed her hand on her throat and grimaced. "You've had a tube down your throat so it's probably sore."
"Liam?" She croaked.
"Is that his name? What you're calling your son?" I asked. She nodded.
"Our son." She whispered and my heart banged against my chest and a warmth spread through me. I never thought I'd want another family, I never thought I would love another woman. But here I was, with a woman that I had fallen in love with and a son that I wanted to be my own.
"He's fine. He's with Cammie, you can see him in a minute."
"What happened?" She whispered, swallowing and the pain was evident on her face. I was about to tell her about the operation and hoped that she didn't hate me for making that decision. At the end of the day I needed to save her life and that was my main concern.
"Hello, Heather." I turned my head and saw the doctor

standing at the bottom of her bed. I pulled away from her, still keeping a hold of her hand. "How are you feeling? In any pain?"
"Just my throat." She rasped.
"I'll get the nurse to bring you some water… Has Mr. King explained what happened?" She shook her head. "You came in with severe bleeding after giving birth to your son at home, we tried to get your uterus to contract to stop the bleeding but it wasn't working, so we had to ask Mr. King for permission to do a hysterectomy as you were unconscious."
"Oh God." She sobbed, covering her mouth with her hand.
"Now, you'll probably be in some pain, but in a couple of hours we'd like to get you up for a small walk. You won't be able to drive or do anything strenuous."
"What about my baby?" She asked.
"You will probably need some help with him too. Most patients recover in about eight weeks, but obviously everyone is different." She nodded and I saw tears running down her face.
"Sugar, don't cry." I wiped her tears away.
"Your hormones will probably be all over the place and your body probably thinks it's going through menopause, so we may have to start you on some HRT drugs too." Heather nodded again. "I'll leave you to it. The nurse will be in to get you moved to a room so you can be with your son."
"Thanks, Doc." I said, shaking his hand. He left and I turned towards Heather. "You ok, Sugar?" She shook her head.
"I can't have any more children." She cried, her voice catching in her throat.
"But you have a gorgeous son; that looks just like you." I told her, trying to keep positive. My phone began to ring in my pocket, I pulled it out, looked at the screen and silenced it.
"Who's that?"
"No one important." I told her wondering why my sister was phoning me. I hadn't spoken to her in almost a year. I'd call

her back later when things started to settle down here.

***

Heather

I was brought to a private room, I was keen to see and hold my son. I only vaguely remember what he looked like. I was still in shock that I'd had surgery and wouldn't be able to carry any more children. I had always wanted a big family and now my body was going to start going through menopause. I was only twenty seven, I never thought my life would turn out this way. I tried to stay positive when I was made to live and work at the MC clubhouse, there was nothing I could have done about it, but if I had got away I would be ok now, I wouldn't be lying here in a hospital bed. Though I wouldn't have met the man that made me happy and made my body come alive when he was near me, I wouldn't have met the man that I had fallen in love with. I snapped out of my thoughts when I heard the door open and the man that I had fallen in love with cradled a small baby in his arms.

"Kade." I whispered as he walked closer to me, smiling.

"How you feeling?" He asked as he lowered his head to kiss my lips briefly before placing Liam in my arms.

"Better now…" I said as I hugged Liam close to my body. "That I have my two men with me." I grabbed hold of his hand and he perched on the edge of the bed and looked at us.

"We're a family." I smiled.

"We are. I love you, Sugar." He said and my head snapped up to look at him.

"I love you, too." I smiled at him. "You can't keep calling me that, when he's older he'll think that's my name." I giggled. He shook his head as Liam let out a cry.

"He's probably hungry, here." Blade said as he handed me a bottle.

"I wanted to breast feed him." I said.
"You can't, Sugar. You're on pain medication."
"Oh." I sighed, reaching for the bottle. Blade pulled off the lid and I offered it to our perfect little boy. His eyes flew open as I placed it on his lips and he began sucking on it straight away. I was upset that I wouldn't get to enjoy having a new born baby again, but it just meant that I would have more time for Liam and he would never want for anything.
Knock. Knock. Knock. I looked over towards the door and Cammie poked her head into the room.
"Can I come in?" She asked. I nodded my head as Liam pulled away from his bottle, I placed him on my shoulder and once he was winded I passed him to Cammie.
"Liam, I'd like you to meet your God mum." I said.
"Really?" Cammie asked, tears pooling in her eyes.
"Yes, you delivered him. You're my best friend. I love you."
"I love you too." She sobbed as she sat on the bed next to me and we hugged with Liam in between us.
"I just gotta make a phone call, I'll be right back." Blade said as he walked towards the door. I smiled at him and he winked at me.
"How are you feeling?" Cammie asked.
"A little sore and upset that I can't have any more children. I always wanted a little girl."
"I'm sorry, maybe if I had got you to the hospital sooner."
"No, this is not your fault." I told her. "It's just bad luck."
"If I hadn't pushed you onto the floor behind the bar…" She said quietly.
"You saved my life. I didn't get shot." I cut her off. I was upset that I had to have a hysterectomy but I wasn't going to let it rule my life. I was alive and had a gorgeous son and a man that adored both of us. I wasn't kidding myself I knew there would be difficult days especially as my body gets used to the changes. I would try and stay positive and be the Mum that my son needed.

Chapter 21

Blade

Heather was finally allowed to come home, we were waiting in her room for the doctor to discharge her. She was sat up in bed feeding Liam and I was sitting in the chair beside her bed flicking through the TV channels.

"I've been thinking." Heather started saying.

"Hmm." I said, listening but not taking my eyes off the TV.

"How does this sound, Liam James King?" My head whipped around to look at her and she was smiling at me.

"You want him to have my last name?" I asked, shocked as we hadn't discussed this.

"Yeah, that way he has both of his Daddies in his name."

"I love it." I told her standing up and leaning towards her to give her a kiss. "I love you, both of you." I ran my hand over Liam's head as he fed on his bottle.

"We love you." She smiled and I would never get bored of hearing that coming from her mouth. I kissed her again and only pulled away when I heard the door open. I looked up to see the doctor walking in followed by a nurse pushing a wheelchair.

"Ok, Heather. Here are your discharge papers and your prescription. Nurse Jackson will help you out to the car."

"Thank you." She said as she passed me Liam, I burped him and got him comfy in his car seat. She climbed off the bed and slid her feet into her sandals and walked over and sat in the wheelchair. The nurse began pushing her out of the room and I followed quietly behind with Liam, who was already fast asleep.

When we reached the car the nurse helped Heather into her

seat as I strapped Liam's car seat in. I had to check it over a couple of times, I'd hate to think I hadn't done it right. When I was satisfied that he was secure I climbed into the driver's side.
"Let's go home." I said to her and she smiled at me and leant her head against the head rest, closing her eyes.

Heather

I closed my eyes once we were in the car, I was relaxed and relieved that I was getting to go home. I was fed up of being in the hospital. I was ready to get back to normality, whatever that was. Would I still have to dance to work off James' debt? Would Prez now expect me to work it off in a different way? No, he couldn't I was now Blade's Old Lady. I was hoping he'd let me carry on with the beauty treatments as payment for the outstanding debt.
When I felt the car stop I opened my eyes and was surprised to see we weren't at the clubhouse.
"Where are we?" I asked looking at Blade.
"Home." Was all he said as he climbed out of the car, ran around to my side to help me out.
"Is this your house?" I asked.
"Our home." He said kissing me. "Are you ok to walk or do you want me to carry you?"
"I can walk. I need to walk, to get back to normal." I told him and he held my hand and led me to the side of the car where Liam was. He put Liam's changing bag on his shoulder and pulled out his car seat. We walked together hand in hand towards the place where we would live as a family. Blade let go of my hand to dig out his keys and unlock the door. He pushed the door open and waited for me to walk inside.
"Wow." I said as I looked around, we walked down a narrow hall way and I noticed that there were pictures hanging on the wall. I stopped to have a look, they were of Blade and who I'm

assuming is Willow, it was wedding pictures and a few of them together showing off her bump.
“Shit, sorry, Sugar. I’ll take them down.” Blade said as he walked towards the pictures and reached out for them.
“No, it’s ok.” I said as I grabbed his hand to stop him. “Is this Willow?” I looked at him and something in his eyes changed. He placed Liam on the floor and pushed me against the wall gently kissing me as he held onto my face. When we broke apart after a couple of minutes I said; “I know what you’re doing.”
“Oh yeah, what’s that then, Sugar?” He asked smirking at me.
“You’re using sex as a way of not talking about it. But we can’t have sex. I’m still recovering. So you can’t shut me up.”
“Oh yeah? Well, I can always put this.” He grabbed the bulge in his trousers. “In there.” He ran his finger over my mouth. “To keep you quiet.” I felt myself blush and a hot sensation took over my body. “Are you blushing?” He chuckled.
“No.” I pushed at his chest with my hands. He took a step back. “It’s the changes in my body, hot flashes are one of them.” I told him fanning myself.
“Come on, Sugar. Let me show you the rest of the house.” I nodded and he motioned for me to carry on while he picked up Liam and the changing bag. I walked through an archway at the end of the hall and came into an open plan space, a large living room was to the left and the kitchen was just around the corner, to the right. I walked towards the kitchen, it was beautiful, marble counter tops that shone with the sun hitting them. White cupboards with stainless steel handles. The back wall was made of glass and a set of patio doors led out to a large garden.
“It’s beautiful here.” I whispered as I stared at the blue sky and in the distance I could see the sea. “Do I not have to go back to the clubhouse?” I asked not turning around.
“Not yet, Sugar. You need to recover.” He told me as he wrapped his arms gently around my middle. I leant back

against him and sighed. "What you thinking?"
"Are you sure you're ok with us being here?"
"Yeah, why wouldn't I be?" He asked, turning me around to face him.
"This was yours and Willow's home." I said quietly. He pulled my chin up and kissed me. "Kade." I sighed; he was doing it again. Avoiding any questions to do with her. Just as I was about to speak Liam let out a wail and Blade stepped away to get him out of his seat.
"I'll just go and change him." He said as he walked off towards the stairs. I took a moment to look around and followed him out of the room. I didn't mind being in the house, but I didn't know how I felt about sleeping in the same bed he shared with her. Something was almost disrespectful about it. I walked out to the hall and looked at the photos again. Willow had long dark straight hair, blue eyes and a tanned complexion. We couldn't look any more different. I did wonder about the baby, she had a large noticeable bump. Where was the baby? Did Blade not keep it? Was that who Lily was? The other name that was on his arm? I heard Liam cry again and I walked towards the stairs, using the rail to help me climb them. The upstairs landing was big, I could see four doors and the one at the end of the hall was open, I walked towards it and I could hear Blade talking to Liam.
"This was your big sisters room. We had it decorated for her. Sorry about the pink, I'll get it changed before you sleep in here like a big boy." I stood in the doorway and watched as Blade changed Liam's nappy, Liam was looking up at him and I smiled as the two most important people in my life bonded.
"There you go, all clean. Let's go and find Mummy." Blade picked him up and held him against his chest, turning around and seeing me standing there. "Oh, hey. We were coming to find you." I smiled at him and walked towards them, I kissed Liam on the head and pulled Blade down towards me to kiss him on the lips.

"I love you."
"I love you too, Sugar." He winked at me.
"We need Liam's stuff from the clubhouse." I told him as he held my hand and led me back down the stairs and seated me on the sofa with Liam in my arms.
"I'll call the prospects to bring it all over." He said as he kissed me and dug his phone out of his pocket. I heard him talk as he walked away. I thought I heard him swear but I couldn't be sure. I looked down at the precious bundle in my arms and was glad that I had him.

***

I yawned and stretched next to Blade sitting on the sofa. Liam was asleep in his moses basket and he looked extra tiny in there.
"You tired, Sugar?" Blade asked, I nodded my head and curled into his side, closing my eyes. "I'll make up his bottle and we can feed him in bed."
"Ok." I said as I sat up straighter. Blade got up and made his way into the kitchen.
"Go on up if you like, I'll bring Liam up." He called from the kitchen. I stood up and stroked the side of Liam's face. I didn't want to go up to bed without Blade as I didn't know where we were sleeping, if it was in the master bedroom I had to bring up how uncomfortable that made me feel. I walked towards him and he looked at me over his shoulder.
"You ok, Sugar?"
"Umm… Where are we sleeping?" I asked, not looking at him in the eyes.
"In the bedroom." He chuckled.
"Which bedroom?" I asked. He turned around to look at me with the made up bottle in his hand.
"The master bedroom, why?"
"Umm… I don't know if I can sleep in there." I told him.
"Don't worry, Liam will be in there with us too." He said as he placed his palm on the side of my face and kissed me

gently.
"No, that's not what I meant… I… I don't think I can sleep in that bed. It was your bed, yours and Willows. It doesn't feel right… Liam and I can sleep in the spare bedroom." I heard him growl and he placed the bottle on the work top and picked me up and placed me on the kitchen work top too. I was now the same height as him. He placed his hands either side of me and leant in close.
"Sugar, Willow never lived in this house. Yeah, I bought it for us and we were going to raise the baby here, but… It never happened." I saw a look of lost in his eyes, I wrapped my arms around his neck and pulled him closer. It hurt a little to stretch but I wasn't going to let that stop me.
"What happened to her? Where is the baby?" I asked as he held me tight. He shook his head and as I was about to complain Liam let out a small wail.
"Here, you take this and go up to bed and I'll grab the little guy." I nodded and he helped me back down to the floor. I was feeling a bit more pain so I grabbed my prescription and a glass of water before heading upstairs.
I walked into the bedroom, it was light and airy. There was a massive four poster bed on the middle of the back wall with matching bedside tables and lamps. The window was big and long and you saw the same view from the kitchen. Hills, fields and the sea in the distance. I placed the bottle, water and pain killers on the bedside table and looked around for something to wear to bed. I pulled open a door to find a walk in wardrobe and all of mine and Blade's clothes hung inside. When did he have time to do this? I pulled open a drawer from the large chest of drawers and pulled out one of Blade's t-shirts; that would be ideal to sleep in. I walked out and shut the door, I noticed another door and pushed it open.
"Wow." I gasped as I walked into an en-suite bathroom. There was a large walk in shower and a large bath tub that looked big enough to fit a family of four in. The bathroom suite was

white and it looked clean and fresh.

"You want a shower, Sugar?" Blade said from behind me, making me jump.

"Shit, Kade, you made me jump." I told him as I turned around. He was smiling at me and Liam was happy laying in his arms. "And what are you doing awake, little man. It's past your bed time."

"Say, I want milk, Mummy." Blade chuckled.

"Come on then, I'll feed him, you burp him." I told him as I walked out of the bathroom and began removing my clothes to get into bed.

"Mmm, Sugar, you trying to tease me?" Blade growled behind me as I striped out of my clothes.

"There's nothing for you to get all hot and bothered about, I look horrible. I can't wait until I can start my yoga again."

"You look beautiful." He said as he placed Liam in the middle of the bed and pulled me closer to him, I was topless and he palmed my breasts in his hands which caused them to leak milk. He dipped his head and lapped up the milk. "Mmm, not bad." He chuckled.

"Kade, stop it. We can't have sex for ages yet." I complained. He stepped away from me and slipped his t-shirt over my head. I turned around to climb into bed and winced as I did. So I reached for my tablets.

"Are you in pain, Sugar?" He asked, concerned.

"Just a little uncomfortable." I popped two pills in my mouth and took a sip of water. I sat up against the headboard and held my arms open for Blade to pass me Liam. Once he was settled in my arms Blade checked the temperature of the milk on his arm.

"It's good to go." He passed me the bottle and licked the milk off his arm. "Ugh, not as good as yours." He screwed his face up. "I'm gonna grab a quick shower." I nodded and he disappeared into the bathroom leaving the door open slightly.

"That's a good boy, drink up all of your milk and then you

can grow to be big and strong like your Daddy. Though, we may have to talk about the whole biker thing when you're older." I knew it was very likely that Liam would be a biker, it would be in his genes. I was talking to him about random stuff, I stopped when I heard the door pull open and Blade walked out with just a towel wrapped around his waist. Showing off the sexy V that pointed to the one thing that I couldn't have.

"Now who's teasing who?" I pouted. He laughed out loud letting his head fall back and Liam jumped and started crying. I placed the bottle on the bedside table and put him on my shoulder, rubbing his back and rocking him gently.

"It's ok, baby, it's just Daddy being noisy. You'll have to get used to that." I quietly said to him, he calmed down and I felt him burp. I looked towards Blade and he was standing staring at me. "What?" I asked, confused by his look.

He shook his. "Nothing, I just love you, that's all… Shall I put him down?" I nodded and Blade took him from my arms. The moses basket was staying on Blade's side of the bed as I wasn't meant to be straining, and getting in and out of bed would be over doing it. I wanted to heal as quickly as possible. I slid down the bed and rolled onto my side, waiting for Blade to climb in. Once Liam was settled, Blade climbed into the bed facing me.

"You happy, Sugar?" He asked pulling me closer to him so I had my head resting on his chest.

"Yes." I whispered. I was at home with my two men, what more could a girl want? "Are you?"

"Yeah, Sugar." He kissed the top of my head as I ran a finger over the tattoos on his chest.

"Will you tell me about them?" I asked quietly, not wanting to ruin the moment. I felt him stiffen and I looked up at him, my hand following until it was on the side of his face. He hadn't shaved for a couple of days and the stubble scratched my hand. I liked the feel of the roughness.

"There's not much to tell, she died." He said.
"Where's the baby?" I was looking at him and he was staring straight ahead, looking lost again.
"She died too."
"Oh, Kade. I'm so sorry." I said as I pressed myself closer to him, nuzzling my face into his neck.
"They were innocent, they did nothing wrong." His voice choked and he cleared his throat. I went to ask something when he cut me off. "Club business, Sugar." I nodded and offered my lips to him for a kiss. He didn't hesitate and slammed his lips down onto mine.

Chapter 22

Blade

"Yeah." I answered my phone as it rang in my pocket, I didn't look to see who it was.
"Church meeting, brother." Ripped said on the other end.
"Any news?" I asked.
"No, CG is trying to find out all the information that he can."
"I'll be there in half hour." I hung up the phone and went in search of Heather. She was sitting outside on a sun lounger with Liam curled up on her chest. As I walked out of the door she looked up at me and smiled. "I have to go to the club, Tiffany will be here to help you in a minute." I sat down on the chair next to her and she sat up straighter.
"Tiffany? Why not Cammie? It's been three weeks since I've seen her."
"She's busy, Sugar." I shrugged my shoulders and hoped that she didn't ask any more questions.
"Is it because of Liam?" She sobbed, I looked over at her and she had tears running down her face.
"Hey, what's all this?" I asked as I wiped her tears away.
"Why would it be because of Liam?"
"Because." Sniff. "She lost a baby." Sniff.
"Come here." I held onto her hand as she held onto Liam with her other one and pulled her into my lap. "Why the tears?"
"I miss her." I whispered. "She's my closest friend." She nuzzled herself into me and I held onto her tight. We sat there for a few minutes until we heard someone come in the door.
"Hello!" Tiffany called out. I looked over my shoulder and she was looking around for us.
"Out here." I called to her, she looked up and waved. "I gotta

go, Sugar. But I'll be back as soon as I can. Ok?" She nodded and I helped her off my lap. I gave her a kiss goodbye and Liam too.
"Love you." She said against my lips.
"Love you, too." I mumbled as we kissed. I pulled back and wiped the rest of her tears away. "See you soon." She smiled at me and I turned towards Tiffany. "Don't let her do too much."
"I won't." She promised. I walked back through the house and stopped to look over my shoulder, Tiffany had Liam cradled in her arms and Heather was laughing and smiling. Her moods haven't been too bad with the changes to her body but I did notice sometimes she got overly emotional.

***

"We have to go and get her!" I shouted, annoyed at the rest of my brothers for not doing anything about this yet.
"Blade, calm down. We're going in. CG is sorting out when the best time is going to be." Prez said as he glared at me.
"Do we have to worry? She's just a sweet bun." Bump said, waving his hand in the air like it was no big deal. My fists clenched and unclenched when he said this, I was having to restrain myself not to stand up and knock him out.
"She's one of the good ones." Riz chuckled, winking at Bump.
"We can go in tomorrow night, I've been going over their cameras from the last couple of weeks and all the Old Ladies leave for a few hours every Wednesday night." CG said as he looked from the Prez to me.
"What about the club whores?" I asked.
"They will probably be there." CG said.
"They'll get hurt." I said.
"Do you remember what they did to Michelle?" Ripped growled. "If they're smart, they'll run." He shrugged his shoulders. Michelle got caught in a crossfire of shooting while she was trying to get help for Heather, she was shot straight

in the head.
"So, tomorrow night then. We'll have church beforehand and sort out the plan." Prez said. He stopped when we heard shouting and screaming. "What the hell?" He asked as he slammed down the gavel and we all left the room.

Heather

"We're saying goodbye to Michelle today, you can't be here." Roxy said to me crossing her arms over her chest.
"Why can't I?" I asked. "I want to say goodbye too." I was looking around, a few of the sweet buns had gathered together, trying to look smart in their short skirts and shirts that were way too tight for them. I was looking for Cammie and I couldn't see her anywhere.
"You're the reason she is dead!" Roxy screamed at me. I gasped and took a step back, shaking my head. I thought she got shot at when the other MC club had targeted the club house, how was that my fault?
"Me?" I asked, placing my hand on my tummy, I was starting to feel sick.
"Yes, you. She went for help, when you were having that brat." She sneered at me pointing at Liam who was fast asleep in his pushchair.
"I don't understand… Where's Cammie?" I needed to talk to her, she would tell me the truth. Roxy started laughing at me.
"What?" I asked, was I missing something?
"He didn't tell you?" She laughed. I looked at her blankly.
"The high and mighty Heather being kept out of the loop. The woman who came to work off her dead husband's debt and she steals the best man here. Michelle's man." She kept walking closer and closer to me until she was in my personal space.
"I… I didn't know he was with Michelle… I didn't have a choice but to come here, Blade chose me." I said quietly.

Feeling slightly threatened by her and the other girls staring at me with their arms crossed over their chests.
"You." She said pointing her finger at my chest. "Are a man stealer… A whore… A fat, washed up excuse for a woman, Blade won't want you much longer." She scoffed in my face.
"Hey!" Tiffany yelled. Roxy's head snapped to look at her.
"Don't even get me started on you." She said. I'd had enough. I pushed at her chest until she moved back. She looked surprised at me.
"You are the whore." I told her. "Not me, I'm an Old Lady. Blade loves me." I said pointing at myself.
"Hahaha, loves you?" She asked, smirking. "He loves you so much that he told you all about Cammie? That she was taken." My eyes widened as I registered what she said.
"What?" I asked shaking my head. She was lying, she knew how close me and Cammie were, she was just trying to hurt me. If something had happened to her, Blade would have told me.
"The Satan MC brothers took her, they're probably having loads of fun with her now." She smiled.
"YOU'RE LYING!" I screamed as I lunged towards her, pushing her onto the floor, which wasn't a great move as I cried out in pain.
"What's going on out here?" Prez roared. Roxy pushed me to the floor and stood up. I cried out in pain again and I saw Blade walking towards me. He didn't look happy.
"Sugar, you ok?" He asked as he picked me up off the floor. I shook my head, tears running down my face.
"Is what she said, true? Has Cammie been taken?" I asked him.
He shook his head. "Club business, Sugar."
"Don't you dare, club business me." I shouted at him. "She's my best friend, she's like a sister to me. Where is she?" I continued to shout at him in front of everyone.
"Bedroom, NOW!" He yelled at me. Grabbing the top of my

arm and dragging me with him. I pulled to stop him and he glared at me.

"Liam." I said.

"Tiffany, watch him." He growled at her and her head nodded frantically as she grabbed the pushchair and pushed Liam away from everyone else.

Once he pushed me inside the bedroom and released my arm I walked away from him to stand on the other side of the room. He paced in front of me, running his hands over his short hair and down his face. He looked at me and was about to say something when he stopped himself, and carried on pacing.

"Where's Cammie?" I asked.

"That's club business." He growled at me through gritted teeth. He stalked towards me and as I backed away from him my back hit the bedroom wall. He placed both of his hands on the wall beside my head and leaned his face closer to me.

"You're my Old Lady. You *do not* talk to me that way in front of anyone else. You hear me?" I nodded. I couldn't stop the tears from falling down my face.

"Fuck!" He shouted as he pushed away from me. "I don't want to upset you, Sugar. I can't tell you anything."

"But..." I started when he cut me off.

"Don't you see, I told Willow everything and the Satan MC knew that. They took her away from me, pumped her for information and killed her anyway."

"Kade, I'm s..."

"No, I don't wanna hear your apologies. You don't get to know what's going on, I'm sorry, Sugar. I'm not making that same mistake again."

I nodded my head and looked at him. "Can you bring her home? Please?" I sobbed, sliding down the wall until my bum hit the floor.

"Sugar." I felt Blade in front of me. I looked up at him. "We're trying the best we can."

"That's not good enough." I yelled pushing him away from me, he fell onto his ass and looked at me. "I want them dead, I want them punished. They took away Cammie from me. They took away our chance of having a large family, a brother or sister for Liam. A baby of our own, made from you and me. They took away my ability to grow a child inside of me, do you have any idea how that feels? To feel empty? To have these emotions running through my body and not sure how to cope with it. I try and stay strong for you and Liam but I'm not coping well, I hate the fact that we can't have any more children. That I can't give that to you." I pulled my knees up to my chest, laid my forehead on my knees and cried, cried like I never had before.

Blade

Shit, how did I not know how she was feeling? She looked like she was doing well, she settled into a routine with Liam and she seemed happy. We were all happy and finally a family.
"Sugar." I said as I hooked my arm under her legs and one around her back and picked her off the floor. I held her close and I sat on the edge of the bed, trying to calm her down.
"We'll get her back, it'll be ok. I promise." I whispered into her ear as I ran my hand up and down her back. She nodded against my chest and I held her close until I noticed that she had fallen asleep. I laid her on the bed and covered her over with a blanket, I lightly kissed her lips and left the room.
I headed straight for the bar, when I walked in the brothers were sitting around as usual. A few watching TV, a few drinking and a couple with the sweet buns. I stood in front of Prez, Ripped and CG who had a deck of cards out. "We don't wait, we go in tonight. I'm not leaving her there another night."
"What about the Old Ladies?" CG asked.
"Get them out, find a way. We do this tonight." I said

slamming my hand down on the table.
"Since when were you in charge?" Ripped chuckled.
"I do this tonight, with or without your help." I growled, looking at Uno. He stared me down and finally he shrugged his shoulders and nodded his head.
"CG, get the Old Ladies out." Prez said to him, he stood up.
"Brothers, church, eight o'clock tonight." He was answered with nods. "Now, where's that baby? I want to see him." I looked around and couldn't see Tiffany anywhere.
"Tiff took him back to our room." CG said as he was tapping away on his laptop.
"Your room?" I asked him with a chuckle. "What's going on there?"
"Nothing, she is sweet and a great fuck." He shrugged his shoulders.
"Umm, Blade I think he's hungry. Where's Heather?" Tiffany asked quietly, looking at the back of CG's head.
"It's ok, sweetheart, I'll feed him." She nodded and pushed his pushchair towards me and left straight away, going out through the front door of the club house.
"Shit!" CG swore, shaking his head.
"Don't worry, son. She'll get over it and start giving you head again soon." He slapped him on the back and pulled Liam out of his pushchair. "Hey there little fella. We look forward to when you join this biker club." Liam was looking at him, his fists flying in the air and his lips pouting.
"Come on, little man. Let's go and warm up your bottle." I took him from the Prez and walked towards the kitchen to get his milk ready.

Heather

I opened my eyes and wondered where I was, usually when I woke up I got a lovely view of either Blade or the bright blue sky, green fields and the sea in the distance. So I was a bit confused when all I could see was a blank wall. I rolled over and saw Blade and Liam next to me on the bed.

"Hi, Sugar." Blade smiled.

"Hi. How's my sweet boy?" I asked as I pushed myself up into a sitting position and saw that Liam was sucking away greedily on his bottle.

"He's good. How are you feeling?" I looked down at my hands, embarrassed about my meltdown earlier. I was worried about Cammie.

"Ok. Sorry about earlier."

"Don't be. It's good to get it all out, why didn't you tell me how you were feeling?" He asked as Liam finished his bottle and Blade put him on his shoulder and began rubbing his back.

"I felt silly, crying over the fact that I can't carry any more children. There are a lot of people who are a lot worse off than me in the world."

"Sugar, I'm sorry that happened to you. I promise I won't let anything else happen to you, or Liam." I nodded and climbed onto my knees so I could steal a kiss from him. As I pulled away his phone began ringing, he handed me Liam and climbed off the bed looking at his phone. "I gotta take this." I nodded and smiled at him. He quickly answered it.

"Everything ok…" Was all I heard before he left the room. I laid Liam on the bed beside me and he kicked his legs and waved his arms in the air, I was so lucky to have him. Some women had to go through their lives never being able to have a child of their own. I felt their pain, but I was lucky enough to be able to carry Liam first.

Chapter 23

Blade

The doorbell rang just as I was about to leave, I opened the door and was surprised to see Wayne and Dwayne standing there.
"What you doing here?" I growled.
"Prez sent us, to watch over Heather and the baby while you're at church." Wayne said shrugging his shoulders. I thought that was strange but I was glad. If things went wrong with the Satan MC tonight I could rest easy knowing that Heather and Liam were protected. These prospects had great potential so I was glad it was them.
"Dwayne, you patrol outside, Wayne you can be inside as Heather knows you a little better. Come on." I nodded my head inside the house and Wayne followed me in. "Sugar?" I called out.
"I thought you'd left?" She asked as she held Liam close to her as she walked around the corner to the hall way that me and Wayne were standing in. "Oh, hi, Wayne."
"Heather." He said nodding his head at her.
"Wayne and Dwayne are gonna be keeping you company while I'm at church."
"Ok." She smiled, rocking Liam in her arms. She knew better than to argue with me.
"I gotta go, see you later tonight. It'll probably be a late one." I told her as I kissed her once again.
"Ok. Stay safe and come home to us." She whispered so Wayne couldn't hear us.
"Always." I kissed her once more before I walked out the front door, jumped on my bike and sped off down the road. I

loved riding on the Devon roads towards the club house, some were small narrow lanes and I could open up my bike and let go.

***

"I sent an invite to the Old Ladies for a new club that is opening up in town." CG said as he watched his laptop. "Looks like they're leaving now." He had hacked into their security cameras, they had cameras everywhere apart from the Prez's office. He had found where they were keeping Cammie, he had seen some of the guys dragging her from a room and taking her back to the same one.

"Let's ride." Prez called out as he threw the gavel down and stood up. We all hurried out of the room and headed towards our bikes. Once we were ready, Prez led the way followed by Ripped, the VP and we all followed in line. There were seven of us in total; Prez, VP, Riz, CG, Bump, Itch and myself.

***

We pulled right up to the gate at the Satan MC compound, Prez pulled off his helmet and looked at the scared prospect who couldn't have been more than seventeen. He went to push the emergency intruder button.

"I wouldn't do that if I was you, kid." The kid hesitated. "Shit is going down here tonight, the best thing you can do is get rid of that jacket and join a respectable MC club." He nodded and ran away after opening the gates for us. No one seemed to be around and we rolled our bikes into the compound and I motioned to stow them away by the back exit. We all climbed off our bikes, the brothers grabbed their guns ready for any action that was about to go down and I had my trusty knife and gun. I wouldn't be leaving this compound without Cammie.

"Blade, you know this compound. Tell us where you want us." Prez said.

"I reckon, Ripped and Riz on the back door." I pointed behind

us. "Me and Prez head for the front door and Bump and Itch, you keep an eye on outside and CG head in that side door while Bump covers you and go and find our girl." Everyone nodded in agreement and we made our way into the clubhouse. We all entered our designated doors at the same time so the MC would be distracted and not focused on just two of us. I breathed a sigh of relief when I only saw two club whores in the bar area. We sneaked up and covered their mouths before they could speak. They tried to scream and I placed the point of my blade against her neck.
"Don't scream or I'll kill you both, got it?" I looked at them both and they nodded frantically.
"I'm gonna let you go, you're gonna walk out of here and never come back. If you tell anyone we were here, we'll know and come after you." Prez growled at them. They just kept nodding and we released them and they held hands and ran for the door.
"Who are you?" Someone shouted, we turned around and saw a Satan brother, Prez didn't hesitate he raised his gun and shot him.
"Fuck, the rest of them would have heard that." I swore.
"Better him than us, come on." Prez said as he made his way towards the hall as a couple of guys came running down it, as soon as they saw us they started firing and we jumped behind a table and used it as cover. Taking in turns to peer around it and taking a shot. Prez hit one guy with one shot and I threw my knife and got the other guy in the throat. "Why don't you use a gun?" Prez complained.
"I remember you was the one that gave me Blade as my name." I chuckled as I pulled my knife out of his throat and wiped his blood off on my jeans. "Besides, now he gets to suffer a little bit."
We heard some other shots ring off in the distance and we hurried to where they came from in case any of our brothers were hurt or in trouble. We saw a couple of Satan brothers

heading towards Ripped and Riz; Prez and I both grabbed our guns and shot them in the head before they got too close. Ripped and Riz spun around, nodded their thanks and carried on down the hall. That was four we had killed already. I looked across the clubhouse and saw CG headed down a corridor and I followed him. Prez following me and Itch following him, we walked into a room at the end of the hall and I saw Cammie laying on the floor, her back to us.
"Shit." I swore as I walked over to her and crouched down. "Cammie?" I touched her shoulder and she flinched away from me. "It's me, Blade." She looked over her shoulder and saw that it was me. She flew into me and wrapped her arms tight around my neck. She cried and trembled and I rose to my full height carrying her in my arms. "It's ok, sweetheart, I got you. Let's go home."
"No, I can't." She said pulling away from me until I put her on the floor. I looked at her, eyebrows raised until she explained. "They'll come after me, I'll put everyone in danger…"
"There will be no one left to come after you." I told her. "Come on." I wrapped my arms over her shoulders and held her close to me.
"Give me a gun." She said. The guys in front stopped and looked around at us.
"No way, she'll end up shooting one of us." Itch said.
"Can you shoot a gun?" I asked.
"Of course I can. I can help, please." She begged.
"Here, we stole this one from one of them." CG said as he pointed over his shoulder at the dead bodies. He handed it to Cammie and she took it releasing the safety switch.
"Watch where you're pointing that, sweetheart." Itch growled as he walked further down the hall.
"Get down!" We heard Ripped shout, Cammie and I fell to the floor as we heard a shot ring out in the air and a grunt. I looked up and it happened in slow motion, Itch was hit, his body fell slowly to the floor and I turned around, my back

laying against the dirty wooden floorboards and shot three times at someone who was heading towards us.
"Itch." Cammie called out as she crawled towards him to check if he was dead. "He has a pulse." We sighed in relief.
"Get a prospect here with a car to get him back to the club house, and call the doc." CG grabbed his phone and we stepped over Itch and carried on, trying to find our way out of the club.
"In there, that's where a lot of them hang out. I was taken in there several times." Cammie said as she pulled on my arm to stop me walking any further. I nodded and told her to stay still, I walked up to the room and pressed my ear against the door, she was right, there was loud music and men talking.
"Were there other girls being kept here?" I asked her. She nodded. I signaled for Ripped and Riz when I saw them to come over.
"What's up, brother?" Riz asked.
"More of the Satans in here… I want them all dead." I told them. They nodded in agreement. Cammie stepped closer as we headed towards the door. "You shoot if anyone gets out alive." I told her and she nodded her head in understanding.
"One, two…" I kicked the door open and stood back while Riz and Ripped sent bullets flying into the room. I heard a female scream, I looked around the room and there was a small, blonde girl tied to a wall. She had mascara running down her face and she had lashes covering her naked body, she trembled as she looked at me. I saw her eyes widening and knew someone was coming at me, I turned around in time to shove my knife through the guys stomach. He gasped for breath and I pulled my knife out and drove it into him again harder. He slumped to the floor and once I was satisfied that he wasn't getting up I headed towards the girl.
"No, please, don't hurt me." She begged.
"I'm not gonna hurt you, sweetheart." I cut through the ropes that had her hands tied together and were suspended from the

ceiling, her feet touched the floor but only just. As she was released she fell and I had to grab her from smacking her head on the floor. "Here…" I pulled off my leather cut and took my shirt off that I had on over my t-shirt and wrapped it around her, she was so small that it hit her knees.

"Thank you… Who are you?"

"We're the Devon Destroyers MC." I told her.

"What are you doing here?" She asked.

"They had my Old Ladies best friend, we came to get her. How long have you been here?"

"A while." She whispered.

"Come on." I held her hand and we left the room. "What's your name?"

"Ashlyn." I nodded and we re-joined the others out in the hall way.

"Let's get out of here." Prez said. "Itch has been collected and Bump and Ripped are spreading the fuel." We left through the back exit towards our bikes.

"You both ok to be on the back of a bike?" I asked Cammie and Ashlyn. They both nodded and Cammie climbed on with me and Ashlyn went with Riz. Once the fuel was spread Bump and Ripped set fire to the building, we watched it go up in flames, satisfied with what we had accomplished.

"Let's ride." Prez called out and we followed him out of the Satan compound and back towards home.

Chapter 24

Heather

I didn't know where Blade was tonight, I found myself tossing and turning in bed without him being there. It made me think something was up when the prospects had come and stayed with me. I ended up watching TV with Wayne, though I felt bad that Dwayne was outside. I tried to convince him to come in but he said he had his orders and he was sticking to them. I thought they would both do well in the club. Wayne said they had been prospecting for nearly a year, so they should get to patch in soon. It would be put to a vote in church. When I started to yawn Wayne offered to carry Liam in his moses basket upstairs for me. He said he would be staying until Blade got back. I thanked him for his company and told him to help himself to anything.

A couple of hours later I heard voices, one sounded like a female which made me sit up in bed to try and listen more. I couldn't hear anything, I slipped out of bed, grabbed the baby monitor as Liam was still fast asleep and tip toed down the stairs. I walked into the open plan living room and saw Blade had his arms around a blonde woman, she had her arms under his arms and her hands were fisted in his t-shirt. His leather cut laid on the sofa. I covered my mouth as a sob rose, I couldn't believe what I was seeing, how could he do this and right under my nose?

"Kade? What the fuck is going on?" I screamed. He turned around, blocking the girl and he smiled at me, taking a step towards me.

"Sugar."

"No, don't you sugar me." I said shaking my head and taking

a step away from him. "What have you been doing? Cheating on me this whole time? Was I not enough for you? You said you loved me." I was rambling and only stopped when she said my name.

"Heather." I looked up and Cammie stepped around Blade and walked towards me, tears running down her face.

"Ohmygod, Cammie." I cried as I pulled her close to me and held her tight. We both cried as we embraced. I didn't know how long we were standing there until Blade's voice pulled us apart.

"Sugar, let Cammie clean up and get some rest." I nodded and I showed Cammie to her room.

"You stay with us as long as you want. You don't have to go back to the clubhouse, stay and help me with Liam." I told her.

"Thank you." She whispered, sitting on the the bed.

"I missed you." I told her, sitting next to her and wrapping my arms around her again.

"I missed you too."

"Goodnight." I told her as I stood up and left her in peace and quiet. I closed the door behind me and as I looked up I saw Blade standing by our bedroom door, arms crossed across his broad chest, not looking happy.

"I think we need to talk, don't you?" He stated as he held our bedroom door open. I walked inside and before I got too far away from him he had me pinned up against the wall, his hands on either side of my head, caging me in. "Now, tell me. Why don't you trust me? What have I done for you not to trust me?"

"It's not that, it's just…" I hesitated. He was so close to me, I could feel his breath on my neck which was sending shivers all over my body. We hadn't been intimate for over three weeks and my body always responded to him when he was close. I shook my head to try and concentrate on what I was saying. "It's only because I didn't know where you were tonight and then I heard a female voice and came downstairs to see your arms around another woman."

"It was club business, Sugar." He whispered, his lips touching the shell of my ear. I reached up and fisted my hands in the front of his t-shirt, keeping him close to me. My body was heating up and I found myself stepping on my tip toes to get closer to him. "I won't ever hurt you, Sugar." He placed a kiss under my ear and his lips grazed me lightly as he spoke. "I'm in love with you." My eyes shot to his and he was smiling at me. I let go of his t-shirt and ran my hands up his chest and around his neck, pulling his lips down onto mine. I was hungry for his attention and my body was calling out to be touched, we couldn't fuck yet as I was still recovering but I was up for other things. I claimed his mouth, licking and biting his bottom lip until he opened his mouth and slid his tongue against mine. I moaned in the back of my throat as I practically tried to climb up his body. He knew what I wanted and placed his hands on my bum and I jumped into his arms. I felt a twinge of pain but it wasn't enough to put out the fire in my body that he had caused. I hooked my feet together behind his back and his hands slid under my bed t-shirt and palmed my breasts. I moaned and rocked my body into his, feeling the friction from his hard on through his jeans.

"More." I panted. He pulled and tugged at my nipples sending waves of pleasure through my body and straight to my clit. "Kade." I moaned.

"Love it when you moan my name, Sugar." He said as he thrust his hips into mine, sending me further up the wall.

"Yes." I cried out. "I'm close, baby, so close." I opened my eyes as I felt him move away from me. "Wait, what you doing?" He carried me over to the bed and laid me down.

"Pleasuring you." He winked. I almost came just from the thought of what he was going to do to my body. He pulled my t-shirt off over my head and ran his tongue from my neck over my collar bone, down my breast around my nipple,

missing the stiff peak. Down over my tummy until he came to my bed shorts. He hooked his fingers in either side and pulled them down my legs. He stood up and looked down at me.
"What's wrong? I know I'm still fat but I'll be back to yoga and running soon." I told him, feeling self-conscious of my body. I looked around to try and find something to cover it up with, there was nothing in my reach so I placed my hands on my tummy.
"Don't do that." He growled. "You're beautiful. I was just admiring your body and telling my cock that he's not allowed inside you yet."
"Kade." I moaned as I arched my back. When he said things like that all I wanted was for his cock to be pounding into me.
"Just relax." He knelt on the floor at the bottom of the bed and pulled me so my bum was hanging off the end. "You're soaking wet." He told me, staring at me. He raised my left leg and draped it over his shoulder as he pushed my right one open so I was on view for him. He licked and nibbled the inside of my thighs, brushing his whiskers along them too. Every time he got near to where I wanted him he pulled away.
"Kade, if you keep teasing me I'm gonna come in like two seconds when you start."
"That's ok, I'll just take more than one." He chuckled.
"Please, baby." I pleaded, trying to move him with my leg that was hooked over his shoulder. He grazed his tongue over my lips, parting them with his tongue. I jumped as soon as his tongue touched my clit, it was so sensitive. He licked, nibbled and sucked. I moved my hips in time with him and I could feel the build-up coming. I wrapped my legs around his head and squeezed my thighs together, the feel of his day old stubble was a sensation I loved to feel. I dug my heels into his back and I arched off the bed as the most amazing and well overdue orgasm coursed through my body. I laid there still for a few minutes, until I felt Blade lightly tapping my thighs, telling me release my hold on him. "Wow." I said, breathless,

smiling down at him. I sat up and slid down the bed onto the floor in front of him. I pulled down his jeans and grabbed his cock in my hand, it was standing proudly. I ran my fingertips over him and he groaned as he got to his feet. He pulled my hair out of the messy bun I had put it in earlier when I didn't want to get my hair wet in the shower. He grabbed a fistful and tipped my head back, placing his cock on my lips, pre cum leaked out and I lapped it up.

"Good girl." He praised. "Stick out your tongue." I done as he demanded and he slapped his hardness on my tongue a couple of times before he pushed it past my lips, sliding to the back of my throat. I placed my hands on the back of his thighs, pulling myself closer towards him. I sucked and tortured him as much as I could manage, I ran my tongue over the large vein in his cock which had him moaning. His thrusts were getting rougher and I could feel myself getting turned on by it, he had hit the back of my throat a couple of times which made me gag, not being able to take his full length.

"Touch yourself. Play with that clit and come with me." I slipped my hand in between my leg and played with his balls with my other hand. "Shit, Sugar. I'm gonna come." I nodded my head and answered him the best I could with my mouth full. I released his balls and wrapped my hand around his shaft and squeezed and pumped him. He held my head still as he exploded in my mouth, there was too much to swallow back and some seeped from the corner of my mouth as I cried out my own release. Blade looked down at me and wiped the bit that had escaped on his finger and offered it to me to lick clean. "You're amazing." He smiled. He helped me off the floor and we climbed into bed. He pulled me close and I lay my head on his chest, my hand was resting on his stomach and he stroked the side of my hand. "Why the butterflies?" He asked, I looked up to him, frowning. "The tattoos."

"Oh, I just liked them." I shrugged my shoulders as my eyes started to get heavy.

***

I woke with a fright when I heard screaming and crying coming from the spare bedroom. I looked over and Liam was still fast asleep, Blade was looking at me.

"Go back to sleep. I'll see if she's ok." I grabbed the t-shirt that blade was wearing earlier and slipped it over my head as it came to my knees.

"You sure?" He asked.

"Yes." I kissed him quickly on the lips before I left the room. I walked across the hall and knocked gently on Cammie's door. "Cammie?"

"I'm ok." She said with a shaky voice. I pushed the door open and she was sitting in the corner of the room, her legs pulled up to her chest and her arms wrapped around her tightly. I walked over to her slowly and sat on the floor beside her.

"Did you have a nightmare?" I asked. She nodded her head and closed her eyes, then snapped them open again immediately.

"Every time I close my eyes I can see them, smell them, feel them." She cried as her body shuddered.

"What happened?" I asked. She shook her head from side to side. "It's ok, you don't have to talk about it now."

"I'm never talking about it, but…" She hesitated.

"What?" I pushed the hair out of her face and she looked at me.

"I was there for a couple of weeks, they never used protection." She cried.

"You're on the pill." I told her.

"But I didn't have it with me… What if… What if I'm pregnant?"

"How much did they?.." I didn't want to say the word, I felt sick at the thought of what they had done to her.

"They raped me three or four times a day. I had a period when I got there, from not taking my pill. They loved that, it was messy." She shuddered.

"It won't show on a test yet, we'll have to wait and see. Though we need to get you tested for STD's." I told her. She nodded her head.
"What do I do if I'm pregnant? Keep the baby? Knowing it was through rape?"
"I don't know, sweetie." I pulled my arms around her as Blade knocked on the door.
"You ok?" He asked looking at me. I shook my head and you could see the concern written on his face. I loved that my big, bad biker man was sensitive too.
"I'm gonna stay in here tonight, with her." He nodded. "Can you bring Liam in?"
"No, it's ok. He can stay with me. You both get some rest." He walked into the room and helped us both up off the floor. He kissed me briefly and left us alone.
"Come on, get in." I pulled the duvet back and Cammie slid under. I walked around the bed and got in the other side. As soon as I laid down she grabbed my hand and held it tightly.
"Thank you for being my friend." She whispered.
"We're family." I told her, squeezing her hand and she smiled at me. I would help Cammie through all of this, she helped me when I arrived at the clubhouse and now I loved her like a sister. I would do whatever it took to get her back to the old Cammie.

Chapter 25

Heather

Cammie had been staying with us for the past four weeks, I loved having her around and Liam loved her too. She still hadn't opened up and talked about her experience and I wasn't pushing her to do so, she was improving each day and occasionally I saw glimpses of the old Cammie.

"Cammie?" I called out as I walked up the stairs with Liam on my hip. As I got closer to her bedroom I could hear her crying. I pushed open her door and couldn't see her, I noticed that the bathroom light was on, I headed in that direction and walked in. "Cammie? You ok?" She was sitting on the closed toilet seat, tears running down her face. I was about to ask what was wrong when I saw the box of tampons on the floor next to her.

"Did you start your period?" She nodded. "That's a good thing right? You didn't want to be pregnant?"

"It's a great thing." She smiled as she looked up at me. "These are tears of joy and relief… I wouldn't have been able to have an abortion and I wouldn't have wanted to have a rape child either."

"Come on." I told her as I held out my hand for her, she took it and we walked downstairs and into the kitchen. I passed Liam to her as I started to make his bottle up and some coffee.

"Are you coming to the clubhouse tonight?"

"Tonight?" She asked.

"Yeah, there is a party for Itch, he's recovered from his injuries. Any excuse for a party. Blade was told he had to go, which means as his Old Lady so do I. We'll lock Liam in Blade's room and I'll have the baby monitor with me, we'll probably stay there."

"I'll look after Liam, here." She told me as I placed a cup of

coffee in front of her.
"You don't want to come to the party?"
She shook her head. "No, if I go, I'll have to work." She looked down at Liam and started talking baby talk to him.
"Uno wouldn't do that, would he?" I asked as I took a sip of my too hot coffee, burning my tongue.
"Uno wouldn't do what?" Blade asked as he walked in through the back door and walked over and kissed me.
"Make Cammie work if she came to the party tonight?" He wrapped his arms around my shoulder and pulled me close to his chest.
"I'm still a sweet bun, Heather." Cammie said.
"No, you're not doing that anymore." I shook my head at her. "Not after what you've been through."
"Sugar, the only way Cammie will get out of doing that is if someone claims her, or if she leaves the club."
"Yeah and no one wants to claim me, I've been there for years." She told me, looking down at her coffee cup. "So, I'll give the party a miss and look after Liam, here."
"You sure?" Blade asked.
"Yeah, quality time with my God son will do me good." She smiled as she tickled him and his legs and arms flapped about.
"You ok with that, Sugar? Leaving him overnight?" Blade asked as he placed his hands on either side of my face and looked me in the eyes. I nodded, stepped on my tip toes and whispered in his ear;
"I had my check up at the doctors this morning…" He pulled back and looked at me with raised eyebrows. "He said if I'm feeling ok in myself I can resume all activities."
"Bedroom, NOW!" He growled. I looked over at Cammie as Blade grabbed my hand and began dragging me from the kitchen.
"It's ok, I've got him. Don't keep your husband waiting." She smiled at me as she picked up Liam's bottle and began feeding him. Husband? We weren't actually married, I was his Old

Lady, but we had never brought up marriage before. I didn't know if it was something that he wanted.
"Get your ass up the stairs." Blade groaned in my ear as he held my back to his chest, wrapping his arms around me, palming my breasts. Once he let go I started running up the stairs with Blade hot on my heels. I squealed as we reached the bedroom and he threw me on the bed. "Strip." He demanded.
"You do it." I said, looking at him. He walked towards me, crawled over my body, pinned my hands above my head, tightly.
"If I tell you to do something, you do it. Or suffer the consequences." He lowered his head and bit my nipple through my t-shirt, hard. So hard that I screamed out in surprise. He climbed off me, looked at me as I laid there. "Strip." He demanded, again.
I sat up, swung my legs over the side of the bed and climbed to my feet. I pulled my t-shirt off over my head, dropping it to the floor and wiggled my way out of my leggings. I stood there in front of him in my underwear, his eyes were roaming my body and I could see the evidence of what I have done to him in his trousers. "All of it." He growled. I reached behind my back and unclipped my bra, letting it fall down my arms. My breasts were aching and heavy, needing his touch. I hooked my fingers in the side of my panties and as I was about to pull them down, he stopped me.
"Wait." He said as he walked slowly towards me. He ran the tips of his fingers from the sides of my face, all the way down my body until he was crouched on the floor in front of me. He kissed my tummy, which was slowly becoming smaller and firmer as I started yoga again, I could start running again soon, the doctor said to take it steady. I didn't want to tell Blade that as I knew he would be gentle with me and I didn't want that. He slowly removed my underwear from my body, the roughness of his hands sent shivers over my body and I

was sure I was already dripping wet. His head leant against my tummy and he inhaled a deep breath. "I can smell your arousal." The vibration from his voice rumbled through my core and I ran my fingers over his head. He pulled back, looked up at me and said;

"Get on the bed, on your back, legs wide open." I nodded as I quickly scrambled onto the bed and got myself comfy. I looked over to him and he was stripping out of his clothes.

"I'm not using protection, I'm clean. Want me to show you the paperwork?" I shook my head, my eyes travelled to his hands that were hovering over the button on his jeans. I pulled my bottom lip into my mouth and waited. Once he was naked, he strolled towards me with that glorious cock bouncing against his muscled stomach. He climbed onto the bed and knelt in between my spread legs. He placed his hands on the bed either side of my head and he lowered himself towards me until he had his lips pressed against mine. I looped my arms around his neck and arched my body, trying to feel his nakedness against mine. I hooked my right leg over his hip and his cock slid up and down my soaking wetness, I moaned every time he hit my clit.

"Sorry, Sugar. I can't wait." He groaned as he sat back on his heels, pulled my hips up and slid inside of me. I gasped and arched my back once again. It felt tight and I could feel him stretching me. "Fuck, feels so good."

"Please, Kade." I pleaded, tightening my grip around his waist, pulling him in tighter to my body. He hovered over me, leaning on his forearms that were next to my head. He started to move in and out of my body and I felt his breath against my neck. I wrapped my arms around his neck, anchoring him to me. He moved his head, kissed me and began to sit up which caused my arms to drop to the bed. He slipped out of me and I pouted, he flipped me over onto my stomach, pulled my hips up and slammed back into me. I cried out and I tried to get up onto my hands and he placed his hand in the middle of my back and kept half of my body flat on the bed. He pounded into me over and over again, his other hand was on my hip and he slipped it around to find my clit.

"Kade, I'm gonna..." I panted as he released his hand from my back and pulled my hips into him as he thrust forward. I screamed out and he drove into me a couple more times and then I felt him filling me with his release. Once his grip relaxed on my hips, I slumped onto the bed, trying to control my breathing. He fell onto the bed next to me and pulled my back up against his chest, we were both hot and sweaty but that wasn't going to stop me enjoying being in his arms.

"Never again am I using a condom with you; that was amazing." He panted in my ear, which caused another wave of hotness to coat my body. I pushed my ass back into him and he growled in my ear. "Shower." He demanded as he climbed off the bed, I was too exhausted to move. He dragged me to the edge of the bed and threw me over his shoulder which caused his release to start seeping from my body.

"Kade." I complained. He walked towards the bathroom and he slapped my ass when I complained. I felt him reach inside and turn the shower on, he placed me in and I screamed.

"Shit, that's cold." He chuckled and stepped in with me. I leant my head back to wash my hair and Blade grabbed my breasts and squeezed, I opened my eyes to look him, eyebrows raised.

"It's what you do to me." He said, pointing to his already hard cock.

"Already?" I asked. He nodded, smirking at me.

"Turn around and place your hands against the wall." I did exactly as I was told and Blade worked his magic on me once more.

Chapter 26

Blade

It was great to have Heather back in the clubhouse with me, she was wearing her leather vest, showing everyone that she belonged to me. It was great to ride in with her on the back of my bike, up close against me. I loved us living at our home with Liam, but this was my world and when she was with me it was all complete. We were sitting at a table with CG and Tiffany. I was drinking a beer and she had a glass of wine, she wasn't going to drink but I told her we could relax and let go as Cammie was looking after Liam. She agreed and I got her a large glass of white wine.
"So, what's going on with you two then?" Heather asked, looking from CG to Tiffany and back to CG.
"Nothing." CG said. Tiffany looked down at her hands, disappointment crossing her face.
"It doesn't look like nothing when she is living here." Heather said.
"We're having fun." CG stated. I could tell that Tiffany was feeling uncomfortable with the conversation, clearly they hadn't had this conversion between themselves yet.
"Come on, Sugar. Let's dance." I said, standing up and pulling her to her feet. I dragged her towards the dance floor and pulled her close to my body. "What are you doing?" I asked her, nuzzling her neck.
"Dancing with my sexy hus... Man." She said, stopping before she said the word husband. I pulled her in tighter and claimed her mouth with mine. We only pulled apart when we got bumped out of the way.
"Watch it." I growled, not looking at who I was talking to.

When I looked up I saw Jess standing by us.
"Hi, Blade." She smiled looking me up and down. I pulled Heather in closer to my side and kissed her on the side of her head. Showing her that I was hers, only hers. "Hi, I'm Jess. I don't think we've been introduced." She said holding her hand out for Heather to shake. Heather unwound her arm from around my back and shook her hand.
"Hi, I'm Heather. You look familiar, do I know you?"
"No, I don't think so. I'm Itch's wife." She smiled.
"His wife? He got married again?" Heather sounded confused.
"No, I've been married to him for three years now. Gotta go, see ya." She waved her hand and walked away. Heather turned towards me.
"I thought Itch's wife killed herself? After she was caught cheating with my husband?" She asked me. I didn't know why they had told Heather that, all I knew was that they wanted her in the club. I didn't ask any more questions.

Heather

I was in shock and confused as hell.
"Where's that little boy of ours?" Uno slurred as he walked over to us.
"My son is at home." I told him. "I've just met Jess." I declared, crossing my arms over my chest. Uno straightened his back and seemed to sober up pretty sharpish.
"Really?" He asked, looking from me to Blade and back to me again.
"Yes, now why was I told that she had killed herself?" I questioned him. I must have raised my voice as the club went quiet. I knew that I wasn't supposed to talk to the club brothers this way and definitely not the Prez.
"Well, sweetheart…" He paused.
"No bullshit, just tell me straight." I demanded.

"Fine, you asked for it. James never cheated on you, we made him say it. We wanted you here." He said, pointing at me with his fingers that a cigarette was hanging from. "We want that baby as one of us… No other club will dare go up against us once they know that we have the grandson of 'Rebel' one of the original members of the Destroyers MC." I was confused, I didn't know what they were getting at. My Dad wasn't a club member. "His blood relative, Liam will go straight to VP. He'll be patched in as soon as he turns sixteen." Uno explained.
"What's going on?" A familiar voice asked. I looked up and saw my sister Daisy coming towards us.
"They brought me here as they want my baby. Am I getting this right?" I asked, turning back towards Uno.
"Yes, the descendant of 'Rebel the Rebellion'." Uno was looking pleased with himself, I looked over my shoulder and noticed that Blade was being very quiet.
"My Dad wasn't a biker." I told him.
"We know your Mum, she liked her bikers and she was constantly with Rebel." Uno laughed.
"Rebel was my Dad, not hers." Daisy informed them. "I'm the oldest. He died before Heather was born."
"WHAT?" Uno roared, turning a dark shade of red. He stepped forward and grabbed Daisy by the top of her arm. "Then you'll stay here, until one of my guys knocks you up. We will have the descendant of Rebel in our club."
"I'm afraid that's not gonna work." Daisy smiled sweetly at him.
"Who are you to tell me that?"
"I'm the daughter of Rebel and I cannot have children." She shrugged her shoulders.
"You're lying." He looked at her and she shook her head.
"Ripped, take her away. I want you all to have a go, get her pregnant." He yelled. Ripped stepped forward and began dragging Daisy away.
"NO!" I screamed. No one moved, I spun around. "Kade, do

something." I heard a few gasps and realised it was because I used his proper name. I was frantically looking around for other Cornish Crusaders members and couldn't see any. Blade stepped towards me and pushed me behind him.

"Get her medical records." He told Uno. "CG can pull them up."

"Na, it's more fun this way." Ripped chuckled as his big hands pawed all over Daisy. She had tears running down her face and I didn't want her to go through what Cammie had.

"Got em." CG called out as he walked towards his Dad with his laptop. Uno read over the file.

"FUCK!" He roared again throwing his beer bottle against the nearest wall. "She's no use to us."

Ripped let her go and pushed her towards me. I grabbed her and wound my arms tight around her.

"Get out of here, go." I whispered in her ear and she nodded her head. The club was still quiet and everyone was standing around staring at what had gone down. I heard a phone ringing and I looked round to see Blade was looking at his phone, he answered it and walked away quickly; all I heard him say was 'Are you ok'. I made a mental note to ask him about that later. I turned back towards Uno.

"So my husband was murdered for no reason? No reason at all?"

"Looks that way, sweetheart." Uno chuckled as he walked away. I stood there watching him retreat as Blade walked back in the clubhouse, he looked worried. As he got closer to me I noticed his expression changed, like he was hiding how he was feeling.

"You ok, Sugar?" He asked, placing his hand on the side of my face.

"No, I don't know." I shook my head and looked down to the floor. My feelings were all over the place. I felt betrayed by my husband as he had cheated on me, but now I know that he didn't. Was I supposed to grieve for him all over again? Was I

supposed to not be happy with my life with Blade and Liam?
"Come on." I looked up to him and he held his hand out for me to take. I placed mine in his and he led me out of the bar area and towards his bedroom. He pushed the door open and pulled me inside. "Tell me what's going on in that head of yours." I looked up to him. I didn't want to think about my feelings all I wanted to do was feel. I grabbed the sides of his leather jacket and pulled him towards me, we stumbled and my back was soon flat against the wall. He saw what I wanted and slammed his lips against mine. It felt like he was consuming me, I felt like I needed him to breathe. I never imagined that I would be an Old Lady and happy to be one.
"I need you to fuck me." I panted against his ear as I stood up on my tip toes. "Hard and fast."
"My pleasure, Sugar." He stepped back and pushed the leather vest off my shoulders.
"No, don't strip me, just fuck me." I demanded. I was curious if he was going to do what I asked, normally he liked to be in control in the bedroom, but I needed this and I needed it now. He dropped to his knees and pulled my skin tight jeans down my legs, pulling my heels off too. Once I was standing in just my panties and shirt he stood back up, grabbed the sides of my panties and ripped them off my body. I moaned and reached for his belt on his jeans, I made quick work of undoing them and pushing them down. He pulled my legs up and I wrapped them around him as he pushed inside my body.
"Yes… More." I groaned. He pulled out of me and slammed back in, pushing me deeper into the wall. He kept a punishing rhythm and my head fell against his shoulder and I kept a firm grip on his neck. I could feel the sweat forming on my back and thought that he must have been feeling it as he was still fully dressed, including his leather cut.
"Come for me, Sugar." He demanded and my body obeyed and I cried out as my release erupted from my body. I was

feeling exhausted and Blade was still pounding away as he found his release. Once our breathing was more stable he pulled me away from the wall and laid me on the bed, removing the rest of my clothing. "You want a shower?" He asked.

I shook my head. "I like smelling like you."

"Crawl under the covers." He said as he stripped out of his clothes. I was starting to doze when I heard a phone ring. I opened my eyes and looked at him, he was staring at the caller display.

"Is it Cammie?" I asked, worried that something was wrong with Liam.

"No, I gotta take this." He answered it saying. "Hold on, one minute." He pulled his boxers back on and walked out of the room. I tried keeping my eyes open but they were slowly closing.

Chapter 27

Heather

I woke up to the amazing sensation of warmth between my legs, I opened my eyes and looked around expecting it to be morning, but it was still dark outside. I looked down and Blade was settled in between my legs, licking and biting me.
"Mmm, Kade." I moaned.
"I wondered how long it was going to take to wake you up." He winked at me. "Now I want you to come for me and then I'm going to make you come again and again."
"Mmm, I like the sound of that." I smiled. He licked from my ass to my clit in one long stroke and I found my hips bucking off the bed, he nibbled on my clit and I was so close. I shot off quicker than I expected when he pushed his tongue inside of my body.
"Shit, that was hot." He panted as he crawled up my body and kissed me, I could taste my arousal on him and it made me wetter. I grabbed his cock and pumped him a couple of times as he moaned into my mouth. He moved his hips so my hand fell away from him, he positioned himself at my entrance and pushed into me slowly, one inch at a time. I hooked one leg over his hip and tried to encourage him to move faster.
"Faster." I moaned.
"No, Sugar. Just like this." He told me as he pulled out and pushed back in slowly. He entwined his fingers with mine and held them above my head. We were chest to chest and my nipples were hard and I could feel them aching as his chest hair tickled them.
"Mmm, yes... Yes." I panted. He didn't speed up, he didn't

fuck me hard. He was making love to me and it felt amazingly hot.

"Kade!" I cried out as my orgasm exploded through me.

"Heather!" He groaned as I felt his release hitting my walls and seeping down my leg. That was the first time I had heard him use my name and it sounded strange but nice. He pulled out of me, rolled over and pulled me on top of him.

"Sleep, Sugar. I love you."

"Love you." I nodded, kissed him once more and started falling asleep as I heard his phone chime. I felt him move and heard him swear. I wanted to ask him what was wrong but I was worn out and my eyes started to close.

Chapter 28

Heather

I woke up to find myself alone in bed, I sat up looking around for Liam and then remembered that he was at home with Cammie. I relaxed back into the mattress wondering where Blade was. Maybe he had an early church meeting and didn't want to wake me. I decided I would get up and find someone to give me a lift home as I was missing my little boy. I climbed out of bed, grabbed my jeans, slipped them on and pulled open Blade's chest of drawers looking for a t-shirt. I was surprised to find them empty. Had he moved all of his stuff to the house? I don't remember him doing that unless the prospects had when they bought my stuff over. I shrugged my shoulders, grabbed my shirt I was wearing last night, pulled it over my head and slipped my leather vest on too. I pulled open Blade's door and was surprised to hear that it was so busy in the clubhouse. When they had church it was normally deadly quiet. Maybe Blade was just out having breakfast with his brothers. I walked towards the noise in search of my sexy man; that had done some glorious things to my body last night. As I walked in, the room went quiet and I looked around and couldn't see Blade.

"Um… Has anyone seen Blade?" I asked. They all looked away and pretended to be busy. Neil got up and walked towards me, Tiffany following behind him. "Morning." I smiled. Neil grabbed hold of my elbow and led me away from everyone. "What's wrong? Is it Liam?"

"Liam's fine. I've spoken to Cammie." Tiffany told me. I relaxed and looked at Neil.

"It's about Blade." Neil started saying. I nodded, wondering

where he was. "He's gone."
"What do you mean he's gone?" I chuckled. "Where's he gone? When's he coming to get me?"
Neil shook his head. "He's gone. He's left. He went about five this morning. He packed a bag. I'm so sorry, Heather." I shook my head, no they were lying; he wouldn't leave me. He wouldn't walk out on me or Liam.
"Maybe he's at home. Waiting for me there." I said.
"He's not there, I spoke to Cammie." Tiffany said as she put her arm around me. I pushed her away.
"He wouldn't just leave me." I shouted at them.
"Believe it, sweetheart. He's left. Gone enforcer again." Uno said behind me. I looked at him over my shoulder. I wouldn't cry, not in front of them. "I'm gonna need that back." He said pointing at my leather vest. "He told me to tell you, you can stay at his house. For a charge and you pay me." He smirked. Did I want to stay in that house without him? How would I afford it? "You can stay here, but you'll be a sweet bun." He chuckled.
"No, thank you." I sneered, taking off my leather cut and throwing it at him.
"Suit yourself, sweetheart." He walked off and I turned towards Tiffany.
"Please can you take me home… To the house, so I can get Liam?"
"Of course." She said.
"Are you ok?" Neil asked.
"Yeah, I'll be fine." Inside I was falling to pieces. My heart was breaking, I didn't understand why he had left, without saying anything to me. What was I going to do now?

***

Tiffany dropped me off outside and I walked quickly into the house, Blade had removed the pictures of him and Willow a few weeks ago. I thought he had done that to make me feel better, to show his commitment to me. Maybe it was so he could take them with him, wherever he was. Cammie rushed towards me.

"Where's Liam?" I asked.

"He's asleep." She motioned towards the living room and I rushed towards him. He was fast asleep, lips pouted and eyelids fluttering. He was having a good dream. He made me smile. "Are you ok? What's happened?"

"He's gone." I whispered, not looking at her. She placed her hand on my back and I turned to look at her, tears running down my face. "I fell in love with him and he left me, he left us." I motioned towards Liam. "Why would he do that? Why?" I sobbed. Cammie threw her arms around me and we both slid to the floor.

After a few minutes, my sobbing wasn't as bad. I explained to Cammie everything that Neil and Uno had told me.

"I can't afford to stay here. I wouldn't want to live here, knowing that he didn't want us anymore."

"What are you going to do?"

"There's only one place that we can go, all three of us..."

"Where?" She asked looking confused.

"Cornish Crusaders MC..."

To Be Continued....

About the Author

Kacey Hamford is a pen name for me (Kelly). I am in my thirties and started this journey in 2014, I love to read romance books about rockstars, so thought I would have a go at writing one myself. I really enjoyed it and got a boost of confidence once my books started selling.

I have gone on to write a young adult series, set in a college. This series is still on going.

I also have an MC series, it was something different for me to write and I enjoyed it so much, especially when I got readers telling me they would love to read books about the sub characters.

I work full time as a dog groomer, I love to read and my friends and family are very important to me. They are all so supportive of my writing career and encourage me to carry on.

For information on upcoming books please go to: https://www.facebook.com/pages/Author-Kacey-Hamford/572126959568554

Other books by Kacey Hamford -

The Rocking Series:

Book 1. Rocking Esme

hyperurl.co/6p848k

Book 2. Rocking Scarlett
hyperurl.co/tjvgpx

Book 3 Rocking Marcy
hyperurl.co/ffymuj

Book 4 Rocking Ashton
hyperurl.co/9hrs7s

Book 5 Rocking Danni
hyperurl.co/tcitkv

Chance Series:

Book 1 - Taking A Chance
Hyperurl.co/puqylu

Book 2 – Giving A Chance
hyperurl.co/h6tezv

15627853R00096

Printed in Great Britain
by Amazon